Angel's Grace

Angel's Grace

TRACEY BAPTISTE

A Paula Wiseman Book
SIMON & SCHUSTER BOOKS FOR YOUNG READERS
New York   London   Toronto   Sydney

SIMON & SCHUSTER BOOKS FOR YOUNG READERS
An imprint of Simon & Schuster Children's Publishing Division
1230 Avenue of the Americas, New York, New York 10020

SIMON & SCHUSTER BOOKS FOR YOUNG READERS is a trademark of Simon & Schuster, Inc.
Book design by Greg Stadnyk
The text for this book is set in Photina.
Manufactured in the United States of America
10 9 8 7 6 5 4 3 2 1
Library of Congress Cataloging-in-Publication Data
Baptiste, Tracey.
Angel's Grace / Tracey Baptiste.—1st ed.
p. cm.
"A Paula Wiseman book."
Summary: While visiting her grandmother in Trinidad, thirteen-year-old Grace sees a photograph of a stranger with a birthmark identical to hers, and begins to wonder if the reason she feels different from the rest of her family is that he is her real father.
ISBN 0-689-86773-5
[1. Identity—Fiction. 2. Fathers and daughters—Fiction. 3. Birthmarks—Fiction. 4. Trinidad and Tobago—Fiction.] I. Title.
PZ7.B229515An 2005
[Fic]—dc22
2003026742

FIRST EDITION

For my mother, my first and biggest fan,
and for my husband, who leads the cheering section.

Acknowledgments

I'd like to thank my parents, Gloria and Roland, who always encouraged my desire to grow up and be a writer; my brother, J, for always looking out for me; my agent, Barbara, for seeing talent when sometimes I didn't see it myself; my editor, Paula, for bringing out the best in my writing; and my very own angels—my husband, Darryl, who makes a great sounding board and takes care of bills and dinner and diaper changes so I can work, and my daughter, Alyssa, for letting Mommy write—sometimes. Thank you all. This is a dream long in the making, and I could not have done it without each of you.

One

My mother told me that when I was born, no one, not even the doctor, thought I was going to live. I arrived too early, and I was so tiny, the doctors had to keep me in an incubator so that I could breathe. And every day, my mother sat by me and fed me and prayed for me and cried because she didn't know what else to do. One day she fell asleep in the chair next to my incubator, and she dreamed that an angel came to watch over me. He was beautiful, my mother said, and he smiled at the both of us and told her that everything was going to be just fine. He put his hand over my heart and promised her that I would be fine. When my mother was finally able to take me home and she bathed me for the first time, she noticed a mark like a small pale hand above my heart. She remembered the angel, and knew that it wasn't a dream after all. He had touched me, and that was how I had gotten better. My mother told me that this was better than a birthmark, that it was an angel mark, and that I should be happy knowing that the good Lord had sent a guardian angel to watch over me.

At times when I felt sad or lonely, I asked my mother to come to my room and tell me the story all over again. I would put my hand over the angel mark, and she would put her hand on mine, and the three of us would smile at our story—Mom, the angel, and me.

I stopped believing in that story four years ago, when I was nine. I guess I just grew up all of a sudden. The story about my birthmark began to seem silly. But maybe if I still believed in my angel, I could put my hand over my birthmark, and I would feel better about this awful summer. What could be worse than being held prisoner on the island where my parents grew up, with my sister and my grandmother? I just knew that Maciré and my other friends were having a great time back home in Brooklyn. I was missing everything.

At first my best friend, Maciré, was jealous when I told her that I'd be spending my summer on a Caribbean island. I pulled the letter I had written earlier out of my pocket.

> Dear Maci,
> Let me tell you a little something about Trinidad. It's a great place to visit—blue sky, sandy beaches, and delicious exotic fruits so sweet and ripe they fall right off the trees. But every day it's the same blue sky, and after the hundredth wave sends you crashing down into the gritty sand, and you've swallowed a gallon of salt water, and the damp and the mosquitoes get to you, and there's sticky juice in your hair from the fruit falling on your head, you get a little bit tired

of living on an island. Two weeks down, six more
before I get back home.

    Your favorite redhead,

    Gracie

"Grace, you get them *zaboca* yet?" Ma called down. Ma was
my mother's mom. She practically lived in the kitchen. The
smell of whatever she was cooking got into her skin, so that
when you breathed her in, you could smell warm baked bread
and roasted sausages, or curried crab and dumplings, or whatever she had just made into a meal.

"No, Ma," I said.

"Well, your aunty going to be here soon, child. You better
hurry it up."

"Yes, Ma," I said quickly. I had learned long ago not to keep
Ma waiting.

My grandmother eyed me from the kitchen window two stories up. Her thick glasses glinted in the sunlight, then fogged up
when steam from the pot poured through the open window. I
took a deep breath and caught a whiff of something spicy and
sweet.

"What you making, Ma?" I asked.

"You'll find out when you come up here with them *zaboca*,"
she told me.

"*A-v-o-c-a-d-o*," I muttered under my breath.

That was the other thing about Trinidad. Nothing and
nobody is called by their right name.

Trees and flowering shrubs filled Ma's yard. There were

guava, *pomerac*, avocado, and bay trees. And hibiscus, orchid, and croton plants brightened every corner of the yard. In a corner at the back was a neat area just for herbs like thyme, basil, chives, and dill weed. That morning Ma had me pick some bay leaves to brew for our breakfast tea. And the avocados were to be sliced and served as a side dish at dinner.

I moved slowly toward the avocado tree. In Brooklyn you got avocados from crates at the fruit stands on Church Avenue. No standing in the mud with a ten-foot pole. I chose a low branch and thrust the pole up. It touched nothing and tipped over, nearly hitting the side of Ma's yellow house. I moved a little to the right and tried again. This time, I hit leaves and brought down a flutter of them, along with the rainwater they had cupped from last night's downpour.

I shook my hair free of water and leaves and looked around. Just past the tree was the mossy brick fence that separated Ma's and the neighbor's yard. If I got a running start I could probably pole-vault over it. I shook the thought out of my mind and thrust the pole up a third time. This time it hit a young avocado, but did not bring it down.

"You not doing it right. You want me to help you?" someone asked.

I took a step backward as a boy from the yard next door hoisted himself up to the top of the brick fence in one smooth move. He flung his legs over, showing muddy flip-flops, and jeans cut off at the knee. He was long, brown, and skinny, with straight black hair that fell down over his forehead, and eyes the color of burnt sugar. "I've got it. Thanks," I said dryly.

He jumped down and stood beside me, looking into the tree. "Oh yeah? Well it don't look so to me, nuh?"

Who exactly did this kid think he was? And how long had he been watching me? I wasn't about to let him show me up. I raised the pole again right up to the biggest avocado on the branch, pulled it back, and swung it toward the branch as hard as I could. It hit, but no avocados came down. The boy tilted his head back and laughed. I couldn't help but laugh too.

"You don't know how to do nothing, nuh?" He motioned for me to hand him the pole, and I did. Mosquitoes were already beginning to feast on my legs, and I wanted to be inside, sitting on Ma's couch, drinking freshly made watermelon juice.

The boy looked into the tree and threw the pole up once. He caught it as it came down, and moved me aside as an avocado landed on the wet grass at our feet, splattering us with mud. He did it three more times, each time bringing down ripe fruit.

"That's how you pick a *zaboca*," he said. He leaned the pole on the side of the house and hoisted himself back over the fence. "All right, eh, America?" he said.

I stood gaping at the spot he had disappeared behind. How did he know I was American? My eyes drifted to the avocados at my feet. "Thanks," I shouted. But there was no reply. "Well, at least I tried to be polite," I mumbled to myself.

I climbed the wooden back stairs to the kitchen with the avocados and dropped them gently in the kitchen sink.

"The tree bearing plenty these days, eh?" Ma said. "How you didn't give the neighbor boy one? Is he who picked them after all."

I pretended to wipe my chin on my shoulder to get away from her look and concentrated on washing the dirt off the avocados.

Ma put tomatoes, cucumbers, and a head of lettuce in the sink. "Here. Fix up the salad." Then she turned her attention in the direction of the living room. "Sally! Sally, come here, please."

Sal, fresh from a nap on the couch, stumbled into the kitchen rubbing her eyes and stretching her long limbs in every direction. Even though she was three years younger than I, we were about the same height.

"You done sleeping, child?"

"Yes, Ma," she replied with a yawn.

"Then set the table, please. Your aunty Jackie will be here any minute."

By the time I had finished tossing the salad with salt and pepper—Ma always said, all you needed to dress a salad properly was salt and a dash of pepper—Aunty Jackie pulled into the driveway. I forgot all about the avocados and raced Sally to the porch just in time to see our aunt squeeze her large frame out of her very old, dented, and scratched-up car. She opened the back door, pulled out a book the size of the Brooklyn Yellow Pages, and waved it at us. Then she winked. A grin spread across my face. I knew that winking means secrets, and I could hardly wait to hear the stories Aunty Jackie would tell us tonight.

Two

Aunty Jackie brushed past the red and yellow hibiscus bushes at the side of the house. Ma's dog, Haysley, ran up to her and put his front paws on her behind.

"Stop that, dog!" she yelled at him. "Gone! Gone now!" Haysley dropped down on all fours and trotted, tail wagging, after her. When she got to the top of the steps, she let the low porch gate bang shut so he couldn't follow her in. He spun around twice trying to catch his tail, and then settled down with a yawn on the top step, like he always did.

"Oh, my, nieces!" Aunty Jackie said opening her arms to us. "Come and give your aunty a squeeze." Sally and I hugged her hard from both sides. I could barely get my arms all the way around her.

"Oh, Lord," she said. "Every time I look at you, Miss Sally, I see more and more of your father. That beautiful dark skin, those big brown eyes, those long lanky limbs. But that smile, that smile is all me. You smile just like your aunty." Sally flashed her some teeth. "And you," she said to me. "I don't know where you get this red bushy hair. That can't be from the

Charles side of the family. I got the whole Charles side in this album here, and not a one of them have red hair like that!" she said.

I looked at Sally, still smiling Aunty Jackie's smile and sporting Dad's long legs. She always got the best of everything. I got whatever was left over, like the dregs at the bottom of a glass of juice. Dad knew it. Everyone knew it, including Aunty Jackie.

"But you are just like your mother on the inside," Aunty said quickly, holding my chin until I met her eyes and made a weak attempt at returning her smile. "Both of you cut from the same cloth, yes? Quick to get vex, and then everybody better watch out!" She threw her head back and laughed. "Oh yes, look at that face. Trouble for so!" She tugged gently at my mane and stepped inside to greet Ma.

"Oh-ho, Jackie, is you then?" Ma said, wiping her already dry hands in a dishtowel and peeking out from the kitchen.

"Who you expecting besides me, Mummy?" Aunty Jackie said.

Ma chuckled. "Come inside, nuh? I make rice and peas and stew chicken. Grace there make the salad."

"Red? You make salad? You know how to find your way in a kitchen? You makin' your aunty proud, girl!"

Sally laughed and pointed at my hair. "Red."

I looked at Sally's neatly braided pitch-black hair, and tried to smooth down my own red bush a little. That girl always knew how to ruin a compliment for me.

"I set the table," she said, turning the attention back to her.

"Oh yeah? It look real nice, baby."

Sally tried to take the photo album that Aunty was still holding on to.

"This is for after dinner, girl. You too hurry, yes?"

I loved the way Ma and Aunty talked. Every sentence was a melody that ended on an upswing, as if it were a question.

Aunty Jackie sat down heavily at the carved wooden dining table and ran her finger along the grooves of a branch laden with leaves. Everything in Ma's house looked like it had been carved by hand out of solid tree trunks. The arms and backs of the couch and armchair, the coffee and dining tables, and all the dining chairs had delicate patterns of tropical fruit carved into them and were polished to a smooth shine. When Sally and I first arrived, we were very careful of them, thinking that they might be uncomfortable to sit in, or they might break easily if we did. But within a week we were as comfortable on Ma's furniture as we had been on our own back home. Maybe more.

As soon as Ma put the last dish out on the table, Aunty picked up a pot spoon and started to pile heaps of rice and peas on everybody's plate. "Did I ever tell you about the time your grandmother caught your mother kissing a boy by the side of the house? Yes, right out there by the brick fence."

Sally's jaw dropped open, but Ma gave our aunt a look that stopped her midgossip, and Aunty clasped her hands and bowed her head. Sally and I knew to do the same.

Ma prayed. "Bless us, O Lord, and these Thy gifts, which we are about to receive from Thy bounty, through Christ Our Lord."

"Amen," we all answered. I kept my hands clasped a few

seconds longer to add silently, "Lord, I hope my friends aren't having too much fun in Brooklyn without me." Then I took it back because Ma always said that God didn't like ugly.

I couldn't believe that my mother tried to convince me that this vacation would be a good experience. So far I had only gotten experience in swatting down mosquitoes in my sleep. For once Dad and I had argued on the same side. There were better things to do in Brooklyn. But Mom said that our grandmother wanted us to spend the summer with her before she got too old to enjoy us. So that was it. Dad caved in and bought the tickets. Even my parents couldn't argue with Ma.

"So, was it Daddy?" Sally asked, wanting to continue the gossip.

"Oh no, no, no," Aunty Jackie said. "Just some boy from school. She was only about thirteen then." She winked at me. "You know how you thirteen-year-olds are, eh, Red?"

Ma grunted.

"Well, I thought your grandmother was going to give your mother licks for so," Aunty Jackie continued. "Imagine, kissing a boy in Mrs. Charles's yard! I didn't think she would be able to sit for a week, but your mummy get away scot-free."

Sally giggled. "What happened to that boy?"

"I don't know, nuh? He probably pining over her still. They all used to pine after your mother. She was a real beauty, yuh hear? But she didn't have much use for any of them. Good thing too, because Ma didn't like anybody we dated."

"Until Daddy," Sally said.

"Well . . ."

"Ma didn't like Daddy either?"

"She likes him now, eh? So don't fret that. Now the two of them tight, tight, like sardine in tin can."

"Why didn't you like Daddy?" Sally asked Ma.

"She said he was too skinny. She said he was like a coconut tree—tall and dry, with a big head at the top." Aunty laughed. "Steven used to look like them bobble-head dolls, you know? Only now that he put on a little weight, he looks like he grow into it."

Aunty Jackie continued on through dinner telling us about various escapades from when she and our mother were younger. Ma's eyebrows arched farther and farther up with each new revelation. But I had the feeling that she wasn't surprised at all. Ma knew everything that went on under this roof.

After dinner Aunty Jackie began to clear plates off the table, but Ma waved her away. She gave each of us a Julie mango, and shooed us out to the porch to eat them because she didn't want any yellow stains on her good furniture. We leaned over the porch railing and peeled the mango skin off with our teeth. As we ate, juice dripped off our elbows and onto the shrubs below. Haysley trotted downstairs to try to catch the occasional drip, but he was too old and slow to have much success, and he ended up licking the sticky yellow juice off of rocks, hibiscus leaves, and his own graying fur.

Ma's yellow wood-and-concrete house stood midway up a hill, in between a small boarded-up blue house that the owners used only around Carnival time, and the Seepersads on the left in their more modern, all-concrete house. The hill didn't slope up evenly. The area right in front of Ma's and the Seepersads' front gates was flattish, and would make a decent place to play soccer, if I had anyone to play with, and if there weren't any cars coming. As the sky darkened and the streetlights blinked on, the sound of someone beating out a melody on a steel pan drifted to us on a warm breeze. The tune was as soft and sweet as mango flesh.

When Ma finished in the kitchen, she brought out a roll of paper towels and the album, and put them down on the wrought-iron porch table.

"Don't touch that with your sticky fingers now," she warned.

"Oh yes, girls. Let's have a look," Aunty Jackie said. She licked her fingers, then wiped them on a paper towel before opening up the album.

There were pictures of Ma, thin and smiling for the camera with family members we had never met. There was our mother as a little girl with two thick black braids that stuck out at the sides of her head.

"We used to call her 'fat plaits,'" Aunty Jackie said laughing. I could see why.

"And there's you, Jackie," Ma said. She pointed at a picture of a little girl wearing nothing at all, running after a white puppy in the grass. "That was right in front this house here," Ma said.

"But that isn't Haysley," Sally said.

"No, hon, that was Thunder," Aunty said. "Hays is old, but he isn't that old. Right, fella?" She looked back at the dog, who had repositioned himself by the porch gate. He flopped his tail once, as if in response.

We flipped through page after page of faded family pictures trapped under the yellowed plastic sheets. There were pictures of birthday parties with kids in paper-cutout hats, weddings full of women in lacy dresses, dancing with men wearing shirt collars as wide as their shoulders. There was our mother and aunt as little girls in bright green school uniforms, at Sally's age sitting on Ma's porch, and as teenagers wearing bikinis on the beach. Aunty Jackie was right. Our mother was beautiful.

"We used to make a lime to Maracas Beach every other Saturday," Aunty Jackie said, pointing at a page full of faded and discolored pictures of teenagers on the beach. "But once or twice we *break biche* and went to the beach during the week instead of going to classes."

Ma raised her eyebrows again. "And I only hearing about this now?"

"Well, we couldn't tell you that then," she said, winking at Sal and me.

"No, I suppose you couldn't. But don't encourage these two to follow your foolishness."

Aunty Jackie pointed to a picture of four men and three women sitting in the sand on the beach. Despite the splotchy photo, I could tell it was a bright beautiful day. Their faces were dark, a sharp contrast to the pale sand and white foam of breaking waves behind them.

"This was the whole beach side. This was Sheila Carr. She and your mother were like this." She crossed two fingers and held them up. "And here," she said, pointing at three skinny boys playing cricket with a coconut branch, "this is your father and Bucky and Jack."

"Bucky?" Sally and I asked together.

"Well, that was just his nickname. You know I can't even remember what Bucky's real name is now, nuh? I haven't thought about these people in so long, eh?" Beneath those two pictures was one of Aunty, our mother, and their friend Sheila posing with their hands on their hips, making kissy faces at the camera. "We looked like movie stars, no?"

And next to that photo was one of two girls posing with one guy. The picture was blurry, but something below the guy's left shoulder caught my eye. When Aunty turned the page, I asked her to go back.

"Who is this?" I asked, pointing to the man in the picture, whose face I couldn't make out.

She frowned. "Hard to tell. You can't make out much in this one. This here is your mother though. See the yellow bikini?" She pointed to another picture that showed our mother wearing the same yellow swimsuit. "This was probably Sheila. I don't know who the guy was."

"But it's probably Dad, right?"

She brought the album to her face for a closer look. "No, hon, you know your father is a lot taller than your mother. This person isn't that tall at all." She turned forward a page. "Here's your dad. See? Shoulda been a basketball player."

"Let me see," Sally said, shoving her face between the album and me. "Yeah, this guy's way too short."

I shoved her gently away and squinted at the photo. "Then maybe it's one of his brothers—Uncle Ernie or Uncle Carl?"

Sally shook her head. "No way."

"They're pretty tall too, so I doubt it. More likely it was either Jack or Bucky, but it's hard to know for sure. Why you ask?"

Ma stared softly at me beneath a frown. Behind her thick lenses it was hard to know if she was trying to tell me something, but the look she gave me was the same kind of stare my teachers gave when they were waiting for me to figure out an answer. I sat back in my chair and let Aunty narrate us through the rest of the album. By the time she was done, it was late, and she decided she'd better get going. She got her beat-up purse and hugged each of us good-bye. Then she reached for the album.

"Oh, can I borrow it, Aunty?" I asked.

"I have plenty of other albums you can look through, Grace," Ma said. "Look at that thing. It liable to fall to dust if you handle it too rough." She turned back to Aunty Jackie. "I put some food in containers for you to have tomorrow. Come and get it, nuh."

"Thanks, Mummy. Grace, why you don't help me take that old thing down to the car. I don't have enough hands for all of this."

I wiped my palms on my pants and picked up the album. As Aunty went inside to get her containers of food I went barefoot down the cold concrete front steps to her car. In the shadow of a hibiscus bush and hidden by the open car door, I flipped open the album. I quickly scanned through pages until I found the picture I was looking for—my mother, her friend Sheila, and the man whose face we couldn't make out. I took the picture out of the album and pocketed it quickly.

As Aunty started making her way down the stairs, I decided to take another photo—the one of all my parents and their friends on the beach. The picture was stuck on the page so I scratched carefully at the edges trying to pry it loose. Soon Aunty was at the bottom of the stairs and the picture was still stuck. Fortunately, Haysley jumped up and put his front paws on my aunt. She staggered backward and tried to get him off her. That gave me just enough time to get the picture out. Just as Aunty got up to the car, I placed the album gently onto the backseat and closed the door. Haysley and I stood guard at the gate as she left the driveway and drove down the hill. "Good boy," I said, and patted his big head.

I wanted to look at the pictures again right away, but I didn't want Ma and Sally to see. So I waited until after Sally got tired from watching TV and Ma ordered us both to bed. Then I waited for the sounds of Sally's light snoring. I stared at the wooden ceiling and waited a little bit longer just to be sure no sounds were coming from Ma's room. A white wood slave made its way across the ceiling. We didn't have these in Brooklyn. In Brooklyn all the gross lizardlike things lived at the Prospect Park Zoo.

I turned on the lamp, sank into the couch, and held the first picture under the lamplight to get a better look. I was hoping that what I had seen earlier might have been a mistake, but now it seemed clear. I blew at the picture to get rid of any dust, and brushed it gently with my finger. There was no mistake. The man in the photograph had a little birthmark below his left shoulder, and just above his heart. It looked like a small pale hand. It looked exactly like mine.

I looked at the other picture from Aunty's album, but I couldn't make out which of the men had the birthmark. So I took out the stack of albums that Ma had under her coffee table and checked each one carefully. Without knowing what the face of the man with the mark looked like, I searched for bright red hair, just like mine.

I studied each picture carefully in the dim lamplight. A lot of Ma's pictures were black-and-white, so when I came to those of people on the beach, I looked at them carefully to find the man with the birthmark on his left shoulder. After searching to the end of her last album, I had still found nothing. I got up and walked around the living room, looking at all the pictures of family and friends that Ma had hanging on the walls. They revealed nothing.

He had to be some other member of our family—a cousin, or an uncle that Aunty forgot had come along, but who? I searched my memory for a family member my parents' age that I'd met. I knew all of my uncles, and Sally was right—they were all tall like my father, and with a darker complexion than the person in the picture seemed to be. Besides, if there were someone else in the family that had the angel mark, we would have known about it a long time ago. Some member of either the Charles or Brewster families claimed every body part that

Sally and I had, every part except my thick red hair, and the angel mark. Frustrated and tired, I put the albums back where I found them and went back to my room. I tucked the pictures under my pillow for safekeeping.

By the time I woke in the morning, Sally's bed was already made, and I heard her outside trying to teach Haysley to fetch. I stared at the ceiling for a few minutes, glad to have some quiet time to myself. I tried not to think about the picture, but it kept popping into my head. So I went into the shower and leaned against the cold concrete wall. Finally I relaxed and let my thoughts go free. A thought played over and over in my head and wouldn't go away, no matter how hard I squeezed my eyes shut to get it out. "You're so different, Grace," it said. "Where did you get that red hair from?" it asked. It was true that I didn't look like Dad at all. And nobody else had my red hair. I tried to shake the thought from my head. My mother and I were so much alike, everybody said so. But my father and I? We were as different as salt and sweet. What if my father wasn't who I thought he was? He and I never agreed on anything. He and Sally were so close, and they looked so much alike.

I needed to figure out who the man in the picture was. If I understood why we had the same birthmark, then maybe I'd understand more.

Three

Days melted one into another in the hot Trinidad sun. Every day Ma sent Sally and me to run errands for her cooking. We went to the bakery at the bottom of the hill, where the smell of warm, sweet currant rolls, coconut pies, meat puffs, and freshly baked bread met us a quarter of the way down. Sally always helped herself to a treat from Ma's change after we bought rolls of *hops* bread, but I wanted nothing. Sometimes we walked up and down gently sloping hills, past old wooden houses made new with concrete additions, and painted a fresh coat of pastel blue, green, yellow, or cream, on our way to buy vegetables from the market. The old market building with all its ramshackle stalls looked like a strong breeze might blow it down, but the husband and wife that Ma regularly bought from assured Sally that they had been selling there for over ten years through heat and hurricane, and nothing, not even the tin roof had blown off.

"That's how long I've been alive!" Sally said with her usual enthusiasm. The old couple smiled, and looked at me, waiting for me to join in the conversation, but I had nothing to add.

My sister also made friends with Mr. Harper, who owned the snack shop across the street from the taxi stand. Sally was thirsty and went in to buy one of the tiny bottles of soda called Chubbys. She discovered glass cabinets filled with Trinidadian snacks. There were local delicacies like spicy and sweet tambran balls, red mangoes, red plums, red anything—named for the color of each fruit after it was preserved in pepper. There were biscuits and crackers, and chocolates with nuts and caramel and crunchy bits. Sally left with a banana-flavored Chubby and a bag of *khurma*. She took one crunch of the sweet fried delicacy and decided to just lick the sugar off them.

Sometimes we saw the boy who lived next to Ma, the one who had helped me with the avocados. He was usually with a younger boy who looked like his little brother. Sally smiled and said hello to them, too. It was the only time in my life that I was happy for Sally's constantly running mouth. Nobody really noticed that I didn't have anything to say. Sally made enough conversation for the whole of Trinidad. And then some.

One afternoon, on the way back from picking up a bag of currant rolls from the bakery, we ran into the boy from next door and his brother again. This time we were close enough that Sally didn't miss her opportunity.

"Hi, I'm Sally. This is Grace."

"How allyuh doin'? I'm Rajindra. This is my little brother, Shankar."

"Hi, Shankar," Sally said. She waved and smiled at the little boy, but he scurried behind his older brother and peeked out from behind his back. "Rajindra sounds like a girl's name."

"Sal!"

She shrugged. "It does!"

"Well, nobody calls me that. Everybody calls me Raj."

He was looking right at me. My armpits began to feel prickly, like at any moment I was going to spring a leak. I pinned my arms to my sides, in case that would help.

"Hey." It was all I could think of to say.

Raj nodded at me. "You're here on vacation from America. Which part?"

"How do you know where we're from?" I asked.

"You have an accent."

"No, you do," Sally said. "We're from Brooklyn. You ever been to Brooklyn?"

"No. The farthest we get to is Tobago," he said.

"We haven't been to Tobago yet," Sally said, and then she rattled off a list of all the places we'd been to in the two and a half weeks since we'd landed on the island. Raj smiled and nodded.

"Come on, Sal," I said. "Sorry, we've got to go," I told Raj and his brother. Shankar waved shyly from under his brother's arm, and Raj smiled brightly at us before he turned to walk away.

My pits were really prickling now. I folded my arms so that keeping them pressed to my sides wouldn't look so suspicious.

"Geez, you're so grumpy," Sally said.

"And you're a little *maco*, Sally. Always in other people's business."

"No, I'm not. You're just—" She searched her mind for a

Trinidadian insult, but came up empty. "You can't even be nice for five minutes. You have that look on your face, like somebody's ticked you off."

I looked down at my folded arms. I hoped Raj didn't think that I was stuck-up, or that I was mad or something. "We can't spend our whole day chatting with people on the side of the road, Sally."

"You just don't know how to be friendly, do you? They probably think we feel like we're too cool to be talking to them because we live in America and they don't."

"Where do you get stuff like that Sally?" It was like being related to an alien.

She shrugged. I looked back at Raj and his brother. They were shoving each other and laughing. No indication that they thought I felt like I was superior, none at all.

Later in the evening I sat outside, drawing a picture of Sally as she tried to teach Haysley to roll over. It didn't come out right, so I crumpled up the page. The sun had just gone down and the sky was that perfect warm shade of purple, a color that usually made me want to wrap myself up in the sky, as if it were a blanket. But I couldn't really enjoy it. The man in that picture kept nagging at me. I picked a fresh page and doodled my family with neat hair and perfect smiles, and me off to the side, with my messy hair and a frown. I colored my birthmark in dark. Then I heard Sally talking to someone. It was Raj. Sally was on tiptoes, leaning against the brick fence so that she could see over to his side. A few minutes later, when the sky turned navy and the streetlights became bright, Ma came out to the porch to see what we were doing.

"Miss Sally," she said. "Child. What you have to talk about so? Why you can't come inside and stop being a *maco?*"

I grinned into the crook of my arm so that neither Ma nor Sally would see. Sally shot a look at me, but couldn't tell what I was doing.

"I'm coming in a minute, Ma," she said.

"Come now, please. I don't want you getting the dew on you. You will catch cold."

Sally reluctantly climbed up our stairs, and Raj stepped back from the wall. I watched him run up the stairs to his own porch, taking the steps two at a time. When he got to the top, he looked back and caught me watching. He waved and disappeared through his front door.

"When it get dark I don't want you two outside hanging over the fence talking to anybody. You want to talk to your friends, invite them inside the house," she said, and headed back to the kitchen.

I couldn't believe that I was getting a lecture for something I didn't do.

"Okay, so I'll invite Raj over then," Sally said. "Now you have to be social."

I didn't mind talking to the kid next door, but none of my friends in Brooklyn made me that nervous.

On Sunday our parents called for the weekly update. I was sitting in the front yard tossing a sticky ball to Haysley, who had successfully learned to fetch it, as long as the ball was slathered in grape jelly, that is. I heard the phone ring. Sally picked up and immediately began telling our mother about how the boy next door was going to teach her to climb a coconut tree, and how she taught Haysley to fetch. Until then I tried not to think about my parents, and what they might be able to tell me about the man in the picture.

Ma leaned out the kitchen window. "You don't want to talk to your parents, Grace? Hurry up and come inside."

I went slowly up the stairs. Haysley followed behind me until I tossed the grape-jelly ball down the steps. I wiped my sticky hand on my shorts, and took the receiver.

"Hello?"

"Hi, honey, how's it going?"

"Okay, Mom."

"You don't sound okay. You having a good time with Ma?"

"Yes."

"Gracie, are you sick or something?"

"No, Mom, I was just running around with the dog. I need to catch my breath."

"Your sister looks like she's trying to get in a whole heap of trouble. She tells me some neighbor child is teaching her to stone down mangos from the tree?" She laughed. "She's not giving your grandmother any trouble is she?"

It was always about Sally. "No, not really."

She sighed. I could see the frown pleating her forehead. "Grace, do you know how many people would love to spend their summer on a tropical island? You have grass and trees and sandy beaches to run around on. You want to be here hanging out in Brooklyn pounding the hot concrete?"

"I miss my friends."

I didn't care about the grass or the trees or the sandy beaches if my friends weren't here with me.

"Write them a letter, babe. Tell them about what you're doing down there. Or better yet, send them one of those cartoons you're always drawing. They're so expressive." She waited for me to answer; when I didn't, she suggested I talk to my father. I heard a scratching noise and muffled voices as my mother handed the phone over to Dad.

"Hey, Grace," my father said. "You not having a good time?"

"No. I mean, I'm fine, really."

"Really? Your mother doesn't seem to think so. What's going on?"

"I . . . I just miss home, that's all."

"It's the darn mosquitoes, isn't it? Them mosquitoes smart, smart. They know foreign blood when they smell it. They biting you good, eh?"

I looked down at the red bumps that covered my legs and scratched. "Yeah, Dad, they are. But it's not that."

"Well, what then?"

I felt a rush of tears burning the back of my eyes. I wanted to ask about the man in the picture, but I felt afraid of what Dad might say. "I don't know. I just don't like it here." I knew Dad could hear the sadness in my voice. Maybe he would try to pry the question out of me. Maybe he would make it okay to ask. He didn't.

"Don't be so grumpy, Gracie, you too big for all that. Anyway, we'll be there in a few weeks to pick you guys up. Try and enjoy it. I wish I had the whole summer to just gallivant around Trinidad. Listen, how about this?" He lowered his voice. "We can have a little anniversary party for your Mom and me when we come down there. What do you say, sound like fun?"

"Yeah, Dad, sure. A party would be lots of fun."

"Oh, is that Daddy? Is that Daddy?" Sally yelled right in my ears as she jumped up and down next to me.

"Is that my little Sassy Sally?" my father asked. Already he had forgotten all about me. It was nothing new. Maybe if I had cried openly, he would have talked to me a little bit longer.

"Yeah," I said, and handed over the phone.

"Daddy? Guess what? I taught Haysley to fetch, and I got mosquito bites all over, and there's a little white lizard called a wood slave in our bedroom every night, and what party is Gracie talking about?"

I retreated into the backyard. Fear was leaving little pin-pricks around my heart, and all Dad could think about was where his baby Sally was. I kicked Ma's *pomerac* tree and one pinkish-red fruit fell to the ground. Now why wasn't it that easy with the avocados? I sat in the dirt next to it and wiped my nose on my sleeve. Maybe I should have just asked my dad about the man in the picture and gotten it over with. But every time I thought about him, fear rose up inside me. There was no telling why. I closed my eyes and put my hand over my birth-mark, like when I was little. After a while a calm tumbled over me and a faint smile rose to my lips, but when I opened my eyes, Sally was standing at the bottom of the back stairs watching me. Her lips were tight and her eyes had narrowed to tiny slits.

"Are you still doing that?" She pointed at my hand, which was still resting just above my heart. "It's so stupid."

I moved my hand quickly, and the smile drained from my face. "You need to mind your own business, Sally."

"Whatever. Daddy told me that Mom made up that dumb story just to get you to sleep when you were a baby. He said you were getting a little old for fairy tales, and that was a long time ago. You don't see me doing baby stuff anymore, do you?"

I got to my feet. "Everything's not about you and what Daddy tells you, Sally," I shouted. "There's a whole world of people besides Daddy and Daddy's sweet little girl."

Her face crumpled, like I had slapped her, and she ran back up the stairs and into the house.

I leaned back against the *pomerac* tree. I had done it now. Sally was probably going to tell Ma, and I'd have to sit for a lecture on how to behave like a young lady. This was the second time my birthmark would get me into trouble. The first time, it was my father who had gotten angry.

Four

I was nine the last time I remember putting my hand over my birthmark. Sally had come into my room and sat on my bed and copied what I was doing. I told her that it wasn't going to work for her because an angel gave me a special birthmark. I told her the whole story just the way my mother had told it to me so many times before. But she didn't get it. So she rolled up her sweater and showed me the birthmark on her arm. I squinted at it, and realized that if I looked at it the right way, it sort of looked like a lopsided butterfly. I told her that hers still wasn't as special as mine, because only mine had come from an angel. Hers was just a regular old birthmark. Sally started making a face like she was going to cry, so I told her that I was sure she had a guardian angel too, but he probably never had to show himself because she never needed him for anything. She went back to her room, and I figured that was that. I was wrong.

A little while later I heard this huge crash, and Sally started to scream. Both Dad and I ran into her room, and there she was, lying on the floor with a scattered pile of books and a broken chair next to her. Dad and I thought that maybe she'd broken something. He wrapped a blanket around her and I put on a sweater over my pajamas and we went off to the emergency room. And all the while there, my dad kept saying nice things to make her stop crying, and telling me that she would be okay so I wouldn't be so scared. The doctors told us that she had only sprained her wrist. Other than that, everything was fine. We hugged and laughed, because we were so relieved. Then we got back in the car and headed home.

Well, by then Sally had stopped crying. She was happy about getting a little sling, and the fact that the doctor said she shouldn't use her hand very much for a week, so she was probably going to get out of doing homework. She started talking, and she told my dad the whole story about my angel mark, and how she had to hurt herself so that she would be able to meet her angel. I was kind of ticked off that she was telling my story. She hadn't even told it right. But then I noticed my dad in the rearview mirror. He had this look on his face, like we had just told him that we'd burned down the house or something. As soon as Sally was finished, he started to yell at me, as though I had forced Sally to pile up all her books and climb on top of them with a chair and jump off. He yelled, "Did you make that story up, Grace? Tell me. Did you make it up?" I was really surprised, because I figured my mom had told him the story too. I said, "No, Dad. Mom told me the story." When I saw Dad's face cloud over, I knew that this story was supposed to be a secret between Mom, the angel, and me.

My dad took a deep breath, and he said in this low, slow

voice that I would never forget . . . he said, "That is just a birthmark, nothing else. What your mother told you is a lie. There is no angel. There is no gift, or whatever you think that is. And you are going to forget you ever knew that story, you hear me? Because if I ever hear it again, if you even whisper anything about it, if you ever make your sister hurt herself again to meet some stupid angel, I am going to slap that stupid birthmark right off your shoulder. You hear me? I will slap it right off!"

I sat stone still on the backseat next to my sister. If she had turned her head to look at me, I couldn't tell. Even my eyes had frozen still. I remember thinking then that my mother had lied to me, and my father was mad at me for spreading the lie. My insides went hard and stiff, and even though I wanted to, I didn't cry. I didn't make a sound. Nobody did for the rest of the ride home. And when we got home, Dad carried Sally up to her room without saying anything to me. So I went into my room, and only then, I started to cry.

I woke up to the sound of my parents arguing in the kitchen. It was very late. Then I heard Sally wake up and she started to whimper. I was afraid that she'd start to cry again, and I'd get in more trouble, so I tiptoed over to her room and crawled in the bed with her and put my hand over her mouth. Well, that made her want to really cry. So I quickly made up a story. I told her that all the butterflies in the world were really descendants of the original fairies, and that they all tried to do good things and help people. Everything they did was supposed to be so good and pure. Then one day, the beautiful butterfly queen who was supposed to be the best and purest of them all was found telling a lie. Nobody cared that she did it to save a human baby from a fate worse than death. So as punishment, they took away all her colors, so she was just this muddy brown color, and they trapped her on the arm of another baby so that she could see the world, but she couldn't go wherever she wanted to. And she had to keep the baby from telling lies and from being bad, so that it would be the best and purest baby in the whole wide world. Then I pointed to the birthmark on Sally's arm, and I told her that the more times she told the truth, or did something good to help someone else, the closer the butterfly queen would be to getting all her colors back and escaping her prison.

I could feel my insides turning to concrete again like they had that night. I could hear my parents arguing again all through that night, and all through my nightmares. I went in the shower and tried to scrub the mark off my shoulder. But all that did was make it bright red, and the mark stood out even more than it had before.

I had never understood why a stupid birthmark would make Dad so angry. I thought about the strange man with my birthmark. Why wouldn't Ma or Aunty Jackie know who he was? Maybe they did know, but just didn't want to tell me. Maybe that was why Ma gave me that strange look the night I saw the picture. Who was that man? The jumble inside me threatened to break my stony insides apart. And then, just like that, a thought floated up lighter than air. What if the man in the picture were my father? My real father. What if that was what all the arguing, the threatening, and the hiding was about? Maybe I never felt like I fit in because I was missing the biggest piece of my puzzle. Could this stranger with a birthmark exactly like my own have the answers to questions I was only just beginning to ask?

I took out the picture of my parents and all of their friends on the beach and stared at it. I looked at each of the men and wondered if I resembled any of them. I thought maybe I bore this one's nose or that one's tilt of the head. It was a stupid thought. How could my father be some stranger in a picture?

I hid the picture under the mattress so I wouldn't be able to look at it so easily. But that night after Sally and Ma had fallen asleep, the picture seeped into my dreams. All the faces blended together and I heard a man's voice calling my name. He sounded anxious, insistent that I answer him. He repeated "Grace, Grace," over and over again. I was mute. My mouth moved, but no sound came out, and my whole body struggled to answer. I woke myself up, and in the distance I heard a dog barking in the same insistent rhythm as my father had been calling me in my dream.

A chill came over me, and I felt all alone in the darkness. I felt like an outsider in my own family. There was Mom, and Dad, and Sally, and I was somewhere outside their circle. Then everything fell into place. I was going to have to find out everything about the man in the picture. And then maybe I could find out where I really belonged.

Five

The next morning I sat sleepy-eyed on the wrought-iron chairs on the front porch, absentmindedly tossing bits of *pomerac* to Haysley.

"I can see your brain smokin' all the way over here," Raj called from his front porch. "You supposed to eat those you know. You don't like them?"

I opened my hand and looked at the fruit. They were shaped like pears, but red on the outside, and bright white on the inside, with a pit like an avocado seed. "They're okay."

"It have a movie playin' in Gulf. You want to go? I'm going anyway, but you could come."

Before I could answer, Sally came running outside. "The movies? I want to go to the movies!" She slid toward me on the smooth tile floor, slamming the chair and me into the porch banister.

"Watch it, Sal!" I said, trying to untangle myself from her limbs.

"Can I go with you guys?" she pleaded, looking back and forth from Raj to me. "Please, please . . . you have to take me anyway because Ma won't let you go without me."

"I'm not going." I looked at Raj. If the two of them were such pals, they could go by themselves.

"What you mean? You rather sit here in the heat throwing away good food?" Raj asked.

"Oh, come on, Gracie, I'm dying from the heat. It will be nice and cool at the movie," Sally pleaded.

Shankar appeared out of thin air, and began to tug at Raj's T-shirt. "And me too, Raji," Shankar said. "I want to go too."

"Not you, Shankar," Raj said. "You too small."

His brother started crying and ran inside to complain to their mother.

"Come on, let we go now if we goin'. My mother will make me take him too."

I needed time to think. I didn't have time for the movies. I made no attempt to budge, even though my legs had stuck uncomfortably to the chair's vinyl seat cushion.

"C'mon, Gracie, please!" Sally begged. "It's so hot, and I'm tired of being inside." Sally put on her best melting-from-the-heat look for my sympathy.

"Rajindra!" a voice called from the backyard of his house. Raj ran down his front steps and ducked into our yard behind the brick wall. He looked at me with the same pleading face that Sally had put on. Maybe if I sat somewhere cool for a while I would be able to think more clearly. Sally saw the look on my face change, and she galloped inside.

"Ma? Can Grace and I go to the movies with Raj?" I heard her say.

"With Raj? By yourselves? Now?"

"Please? It's okay, right?"

"Well, I guess it's all right. You all be careful, eh?" Ma said, emerging from the house wiping her hands on a dishtowel. "How you getting there? You walking? It's not that far, you know. Just don't take them maxi-taxi and them. All they care about is the couple of dollars they can make off of you. They could care less if you arrive alive or dead, wherever you going."

"Yes, Ma," I said. Sally ran out and headed down the front steps, dragging me with her.

"Be careful!" Ma called out.

"Yes, Ma," we said in unison.

We snuck out through the gate with Raj, and ducked as we went past his house. Then we opened up, and ran until we got over the hill and all the way to the taxi stand. At the corner where the regular taxis and the maxi-taxi vans lined up, we stopped, hunched over with our hands on our knees and panted to catch our breath.

"You think your mother saw us?" Sally asked.

Raj shook his head. "She probably still calling 'Rajindra! Rajindra!'" he said in a funny voice. We burst into laughter and doubled over again, gasping for air.

"Come on," he said between puffs of breath. "Let's go." He headed toward the maxi-taxi side of the stand.

"Wait. I told Ma we wouldn't take those," I said.

"Oh, come on. It can't be that bad," Sally protested. "Look how many people take them. Besides, they're prettier."

She pointed at the stripes painted along the sides of every

maxi-taxi. The drivers had also personalized their vehicles with names like "Lightning Flash" and "Stealth Rider." Some even had logos painted on their sides.

"Why are they different colors?" I asked.

"The colors tell you where you're going. Like the green ones take you to Port of Spain and the brown ones take you through La Romain. We need a brown one." He started looking around for the right color maxi to take us where we needed to go. He stepped into the crowd, bobbing and weaving to get through. Sally and I followed behind.

I didn't want to disobey Ma, especially since I figured she could smell the lie on you. And most of the maxi vans looked really old and beat-up. "I don't know. Ma really didn't want us to take a maxi."

"We not going that far," Raj assured me. "Fifteen minutes tops." He smiled, and I followed as he ushered Sal and me into a brown-striped maxi with a cardboard sign on the dashboard that read LA ROMAIN/GULF CITY MALL. We squeezed into the back-seat and waited until the maxi was full. Then a tall man with his thin, shoulder-length dreadlocks tied back with a rubber band hopped into the driver's seat and we took off. The maxi-taxi pelted through the streets filled with cars and people. We passed houses with silver, green, or red tin roofs, businesses with their names and phone numbers painted right on the front walls, and stray dogs lazing about in the sun everywhere. We raced up and down hills, and through narrow curvy roads. Every few feet the driver jerked to a stop to drop off and pick up passengers.

There were no seat belts, so I grabbed on to the cracked seat and said a silent prayer like Ma had taught me. Ma was right. These things were death traps. But soon enough the driver screeched to a halt in front of a quarter-mile-long multicolored building and announced the destination.

"Gulf!"

I put my hand above my heart and tried to catch my breath. Sally looked back at me, and I moved my hand immediately. I tried to see her face to figure out if she had seen that I had touched my birthmark, but she had turned away from me just in time. As the three of us got out of the maxi, the driver sped off again. I didn't know about Sal and Raj, but I was definitely going to walk back home.

Sally raced ahead of Raj and me. As she opened the doors to the mall, cool air washed over us like a wave and pulled us into the building.

"I am going over there!" Sally said, pointing at a music store. She sprinted ahead and disappeared almost immediately into the crowd. Raj and I scrambled after her to make sure we didn't lose her in the crowd.

"You can't do that, Sal!" I said, grabbing her by the arm. "You can't just go off on your own. You don't even know where you are."

She shrugged me off, and walked more slowly toward the store. "I told you where I was going. Geez!"

I continued to follow her, but Raj touched my shoulder to stop me. "We'll pick up the tickets, all right?" he said to her back. "The movie startin' half-eleven. That's in forty-five minutes. You just wait here for us, and we will come back and get you, right?"

"I'll need to get popcorn and soda."

"Okay," Raj said. "Thirty minutes. Don't go anywhere else, okay?" He wasted a perfectly white smile on her, but then turned it toward me. "Come on, I'll show you the scenic route."

We walked past a store with mannequins wearing saris, an ice-cream parlor selling all kinds of flavors including soursop, passion fruit, papaya, and mango, and a store that sold carved statues and intricate boxes made of wood and brass.

"What's—"

"You don't say much," Raj said, catching me midsentence. We laughed. "Sorry, what you were going to say?"

I shook my head. "Nothing. Why do you think I don't say much?"

"You don't. Your sister does all the talking."

"That's why I don't say much. I can't get a word in when she's around."

"Well, she's not here now," he said with a grin.

There was a table outside the store with wooden animals, and figures in fancy costumes doing dance poses. Some had several pairs of arms. I picked up a small box with a carving of a man with an elephant's head and looked at it.

"That's Ganesha," Raj said. "He's an Indian deity."

"What's he for?"

"What you mean 'for'?"

"I mean, what does he do? You know how there are saints

that you can pray to for traveling, or even for helping to find stuff you've lost."

"He's for knowledge, or wisdom, or something like that, but I don't really know for sure, nuh? We're not Hindu anymore. My mother converted when I was real little. I remember some stuff, but not a lot."

"Why'd you stop being Hindu?"

"We became Christian after my mother and father split up, and we moved in with Harry. He's Christian."

"Harry? Your dad? You mean he's not your real father? And you call him 'Harry'? To his face?"

He grinned. "No, I don't call him that when he's around."

"Oh." I put down the box and we started to walk again. "So how long have you lived with him?"

"We moved in with him when Shankar was still a baby."

"So does Shankar know about Harry?"

"Know what?"

"That Harry isn't your real dad."

He shrugged.

"Well, don't you think your mom or someone should tell him?"

"What he need to know that for? He too young for all that."

"But don't you think that's lying? Don't you think he'd want to know about his read dad?"

"No."

"Well, I don't think that's up to you to decide."

"I don't think that's for you to decide either."

"Well, what I mean is, if I don't tell my mother everything, she tells me that 'omission is just as bad as lying.' I'm just saying that if Shankar ever finds out, he'll think that you guys have lied to him all this time."

"Parents must have a manual or something. My mother like to tell me the same thing too."

"But she's still lying to your brother."

He stopped walking. The perfect smile was gone from his face, and the lock of dark hair covering his eyes made it impossible to tell if he was just a little upset, or really angry. I felt stupid for saying anything at all. "You think my father is somebody Shankar would really want to know? You don't know my father. Anyway, parents lie all the time themselves. It's 'do as I say, but not as I do.' You know? My mother used to tell me that my father was going to stop beating her every time he got drunk off his paycheck. And every time my father woke up sober, he used to promise he would never drink again." He leaned against a railing and looked out at nothing in particular. "Parents lie to you because they think you'll be better off not knowing the truth." He breathed heavily. "Or else they do it because they want to believe their own lie. I learn that long time, eh? You think your parents never make up stories to tell you? Believe me, they have, even if it was just about the tooth fairy. Just because they grown doesn't mean that they any better at telling the truth."

The truth. It had never occurred to me that the truth might be so bad, that it might be an alcoholic father, or a deadbeat dad, or worse, someone who had hurt my mother.

"I'd still rather know the truth," I whispered.

"You can afford to say that because you don't have nothing

to worry about. You never had to duck down behind cars in the street so your father wouldn't see you and embarrass you in front of your friends or take a swing at you. The truth is not for everybody."

"You don't know anything about me. How do you know what I have or don't have to worry about?"

"Oh, is so? So what's your big secret then? I've been watching you staring into space all morning. You're like Chicken Little, waiting for the sky to drop. I bet whatever it is, ain't half as bad as you think." He pointed at my frown and smiled, unveiling two rows of perfect white teeth.

I couldn't help but smile back. "I can't say."

"You can't say because you don't know, or you don't want to say?"

"I just can't say. It's really personal. That's why."

He sucked his teeth. "It can't be any more personal than what I just told you."

Could I trust the boy who just told me that his father was an alcoholic who beat his mother? He made me want to tell him everything about me, but I was embarrassed. He thought I had the perfect family. Now he would know that it wasn't true. At least he knew who his father was. And his mother had left for a very good reason. My own mother's reasons remained as mysterious to me as the man in the picture. I put my hands in my pocket, where I carried the two pictures from Aunty Jackie's album. Because Sally was known for sneaking up and snooping around, I couldn't risk leaving them anywhere in Ma's house, not even under my own mattress. I wished I were back in Brooklyn, where I had friends that I could talk to. But I wasn't. They were far away, and right in front of me, Raj's smile seemed trustworthy and encouraging.

I pulled the pictures out and handed them to him. He looked at them carefully. I pointed at the birthmark on the man in the first photo, and pulled aside the strap of my tank top to show him my matching one.

"I have no idea who this person is, but we have the same birthmark."

Raj waited, trying to understand my point.

"I think he may be my real father. No one in my family has that birthmark. Just me."

"You can't know everything about everybody in your family. Did you ever ask if anybody had the same birthmark as you?"

"No."

"Why not?"

I looked down. I didn't want to think about the angel story again. That always got me in trouble. "Look, there's no other explanation for it."

"How you going to find out if he really is your father then?"

"Well my aunt said that when she and my mom were younger, they used to have beach parties all the time. She had a bunch of pictures. These two were taken the same day. She said that this second one is of everybody that was there that day. So my father has to be one of these men."

He raised his eyebrows. "Huh. What you going to do now?"

"I don't know. If I start asking questions, Ma will know

what I'm doing and she'll tell my parents for sure. Then I'll never find out anything."

"You think your grandmother knows?"

"There isn't a lot Ma doesn't know."

He nodded. "Why don't you just ask her then?"

"I thought about that, but obviously they don't want me to know, so I'm going to have to find out myself."

"I guess that's why you think I should tell my brother about my father."

"Well, maybe that's different. You said your dad was pretty awful."

"So why don't you think that could be the same for you?"

"I guess it could be, but I'd still rather find out for myself, and I have to find out soon. My parents will be back in five weeks, and then—"

"Then we're going to have a party," Sally said, slipping alongside Raj.

"Sally! I told you to wait at the music store. How long have you been standing there? Were you eavesdropping again?"

"I don't eavesdrop, Grace. I can't help it if you're so loud that I can hear you a mile away." She made a face at me, and grinned when I looked angry. "Besides, the two of you took too long. You said you'd be back in thirty minutes, and it's almost time for the movie to start." She tapped the face of her watch. "So do you want to come to the party?" she asked Raj.

"Sure."

"Great. Who else do you think we should invite, Gracie?" She began to count off people on her fingers. "Ma, Aunty

Jackie, Raj, Raj's mom, Shankar, Raj's dad."

"Dad said a little party, Sally."

"What if we had a beach party like the ones they used to have with their friends?" she asked, ignoring me completely. "Wouldn't that be great, Gracie? We could get those bake and shark sandwiches, like when we went to Maracas Beach with Aunty Jackie. Oh, we should go to Maracas!"

"If you inviting a whole bunch of people, maybe you should invite some of your parents' old friends, too," Raj said.

"That's a good idea," Sally said. "Like those people in Aunty Jackie's photo album."

Raj nodded at me, and we shared a smile.

"We could get Aunty Jackie to call them for us," Sally said.

"Well, Aunty Jackie's busy working. Maybe we should call them ourselves, Sal."

"Yeah, okay. Yaay!" Sally yelled, skipping ahead to the movie theater's ticket booth.

I couldn't help but smile. Maybe this wasn't going to be as hard as I thought. I caught Raj raising his eyebrows at me.

"What's the difference if you call or your aunt calls?" he asked.

"If Sal and I call, I'll get a chance to talk to everyone and try to figure it out before my parents get here." He nodded. "Thanks, Raj. That was really smart, what you did." He winked at me, and I tried hard not to grin. We were sharing a secret. I was glad I had told him about my father. And Ma would never suspect that I was trying to find out anything, because Sally would take the credit for everything. Raj handed the pictures back to me. He turned toward the movie theater, where Sally was already chatting up the guy in the ticket booth.

"Hold on one sec," I said.

I ran in the opposite direction, toward a bookstore. I went in and got a postcard with a picture of a flock of scarlet ibis, and a stamp. I got out my pen and scrawled quickly.

Dear Maci,

Maybe Trinidad isn't so bad. There's a kid who lives next door to my grandmother. His name is Raj. He's our age. He's really nice. But I still miss being home. There's so much other stuff going on, but I can't tell you now. Write back!

Love,

Gracie

Now I just had to find a mailbox to drop it off. In the meantime, I put it in my pocket and ran back out to meet my sister and my new friend.

Six

Sally shared the plan with Ma and our aunt the following night. Aunty Jackie liked the beach party idea immediately. Ma was another story.

"I guess I could make it out in the hot sun for one day," she said. "I think I have a big straw hat somewhere. It old, but it will do." Ma turned her back to us and continued to chop *caraili* on the counter.

"Oh God, Mummy," Aunty Jackie said. "You could give trouble, yes? Why you have to be so?"

"My old bones ent make for that kind of thing again." Ma ended her sentence by dropping a piece of ginger to sizzle in a pan of hot oil. Then she added seasoned meat and the *caraili*.

"I didn't know when you get old you turn vampire. You think the sun will kill you, Mummy?" Aunty Jackie said, trying to get her back into the conversation.

"Oh please, Ma?" Sally whined. "We need you there or it won't be fun. Mom probably won't go if you don't want to, and then we won't have a party like Daddy wanted."

"All right, all right. But just leave me under a coconut tree with my hat and my umbrella, and let me know when you ready to go back home." Ma turned back to her pot and tended to it with one hand while the other rested firmly on her hip. "I not able with you young people, nuh?" she mumbled.

My body tensed as I waited for Sally to tell them who she was planning to invite.

"And why you so quiet?" Ma asked me over her shoulder.

I shrugged. "I'm not quiet. I'm listening."

"She's quiet because I'm in charge," Sally said.

"I know you grinning back there, Miss Grace," she said. "You all up to something. You two think you grown."

"Well, actually there is something else. I need Aunty Jackie to help me find everybody so I can invite them," Sally said.

"Who everybody?" Ma asked. "Besides your parents, everybody is in this room."

Sally shook her head, and her eyes sparkled like someone about to tell a juicy secret.

"Well, who you think you inviting, then?"

"You, Aunty, Grace, Raj and his family, and all of Mom and Dad's friends."

"Which friends you talking about?" Ma asked.

"The ones from Aunty Jackie's pictures," Sally said.

"What you all talking about? I know you not saying you want to dig up all them people for a little party."

Sally nodded vigorously. "Yup. We do."

Ma shot me a look. "Eh-eh," she said, shaking her head. "Your father said a little party. You not going looking for all these people when you not even sure your parents want to see them, not if I have anything to do with it."

"Oh come on, Mummy," Aunty Jackie pleaded. "Look how excited they are about their little party. What could it hurt for them to have their fun?"

"Jackie, what I tell you about encouraging these girls in foolishness? You all want to stir up trouble, and I am not standing for it."

"We won't be any trouble at all," Sally said. "We won't pester anybody. Promise."

Ma's gray head was still shaking slowly side to side. She stirred the pot in time with her head. For the first time since we arrived that summer, she looked tired. I was just about to call off the whole party when Ma said, "If you determined to go through with this thing, I can't stop you. Do what you want." Even though she wasn't looking at any of us, I felt that Ma was talking directly to me. Goose bumps prickled up on my arms.

Sally broke into a grin and jumped up and down. "Thank you, Ma," she said, hugging our grandmother.

Aunty Jackie motioned for us to follow her out to the living room. We both knew not to involve Ma in any more of the party plans.

"So where we going to find all those people?" Aunty asked. "I haven't seen any of them in years. Your parents even remember where to find these folks?" She looked at Sally and me. "Well, I guess when they call on Sunday we could ask whose number they have."

"No!" Sally shouted. "It has to be a surprise. We can't tell them who's coming."

"Well, I think this is real nice, girls," Aunty said. "But it won't be much of a surprise since it was your father's idea to have a party in the first place."

"The surprise is that all their old friends are coming, Aunty. We can't let them know that part, okay?"

"Then you shouldn't have told me. Lord knows I can't keep a secret. But all right, I will see who I can remember."

"It has to be the same," Sally insisted. "Maybe if you look at the pictures again you will remember everybody?"

My body tensed.

"Well, is a good thing I didn't take that album out the car yet."

"I'll get it," I volunteered. I grabbed Aunty's car keys and ran into the bedroom. I got my slippers. Then I took the pictures out from my new hiding place under the lining of the drawer in my nightstand and ran out to the car. I replaced them carefully in the album and headed back upstairs.

"How you breathing so hard, girl? You didn't run that far!" Aunty said as I handed her the album. I tried to control my breathing as Aunty Jackie turned to the page with pictures of everyone on the beach. She took a careful look. "Well, I think Sheila got married to some fella up north. 'Jarvis' I think. We could look up Sheila Jarvis in the phone book and hope the number is under her name. Maybe she can help you find the rest of them, 'cause Lord knows I can't. It's been real long since I've seen any of them. It will be nice to have everybody together again, though." She slapped Sally on the shoulder. "What a nice present. Your parents are lucky to have such thoughtful children." Sally beamed and, for once, said nothing. "I'll look up Sheila in the phone book and give her a call."

"That's okay, Aunty," I said. "You don't have to. Sally and I will take care of that. We just need everybody's names, that's all. And maybe we should hold on to the pictures, too—you know, for reference."

She tried to smooth down my thick mane. "You girls are real sweet, eh?"

Late that night, after we had settled into bed, the sound of distant dogs barking surrounded us, and Sally piped up again.

"We should get blindfolds."

I cocked my head in her direction, but didn't open my eyes. I heard her bed creak as she turned to face me.

"You know, so they won't know where we're going."

"I think the smell of salt water and the sound of the waves will give them a hint, Sal."

"Yeah, but they won't know right away. Or maybe we can surprise them that morning at breakfast."

"Well, at least then they'd know to wear their swimsuits."

"It's going to be so much fun. We can play games in the sand, and Ma will make a big pot of food, and we'll drink coconut water right out of the coconuts."

"Go to sleep, Sal!"

In the morning I flipped through the album as Sally looked through the phone book for Sheila Jarvis. I wondered how I would know which one of the men was my father. Maybe when I spoke to one of them on the phone to invite him to the party, and when I said "I'm Christine Charles's daughter," he'd stammer or clear his throat, and I'd know instantly that I had found him. When he got over the surprise, his voice would be deep and soothing, and he would say that he was looking forward to meeting me. Then at the beach, he would smile brightly and wave, and I would recognize him from the birthmark on his shoulder. He would give me a huge hug and tell me how pretty I was, and that my hair was as thick and red as his mother's.

I looked up from the album and saw Raj's house through the living-room window. If my father was really so nice and knew all about me, then why hadn't I heard from him before? Maybe my father left my mother and ran off and nobody knew where he was. Maybe he didn't want to have anything to do with my mother after he found out about me. Maybe that was why Aunty Jackie hadn't seen him in so long. If I found my real father, would my mother get hurt, or angry? Maybe my dad would be the one who got hurt, finding out that I'm not really his. If my real father suddenly showed up in our lives, would it be the end of my family?

Sally plopped the phone book in my lap and pointed at a number for "Jarvis, Sheila." I shoved the book off my lap. It landed with a thud on Ma's wooden floor.

"Sal! You can't just drop five-pound books on people! What's the matter with you?" I got up and went into the bathroom and leaned against the door. Why hadn't I thought of it before? Raj was right. The truth isn't for everybody. All this time my mother might have been trying to protect me from someone awful. I rubbed the heel of my palms into my eyes. I had to stop being so negative. It mightn't be so bad. I had to stop making up these stories in my head.

When I came back to the living room, Sally was sitting on the couch with a glum face, looking up the number again. She pulled the phone to the table and began to dial.

"Wait, Sal," I said. "She's probably at work now. I'll call her later, okay?"

"Sorry I dropped the book on you, Gracie."

"That's okay. I'm sorry I yelled at you."

"Apology accepted."

Ma poked her head out of the kitchen. "The two of you done quarreling? Good. I need to get some sweet peppers from the vegetable stand." She took her purse off the counter and took out some money. "Here. And you can use the extra to get a little something for yourself."

"Thanks, Ma," I said. "Green or red?"

"Yellow peppers, if they have them, but either red or green will do if they don't."

Sally and I headed out. We met Raj and Shankar coming from the opposite direction.

"We're going to get some peppers for Ma," Sally said.

"We just came from there," Raj said. He held up a bunch of pea pods in a clear plastic bag to show us. "Hold on, okay?"

He ran into his house and dropped off the bag as Sally and Shankar ran ahead. When he came back, I told him about what was worrying me.

"I was thinking about what you told me about your dad— your real dad. What if this person, my real father, isn't what I think he is?"

"What you mean?"

"I mean what if he's like your—" I stopped myself. "What if he hit my mother or something? What if he never wanted me in the first place?"

"You know, you not going to know for sure if you don't go looking for him." He flicked hair out of his eyes. "I know it's scary."

"No. Well, yeah, I guess."

"Look, sometimes the truth not so good to know about. But how you going to know for sure, if you don't try to find out. He might be nice."

"But what if he isn't?"

Raj shrugged. "What if somewhere down the road you realize you really want to know who the man is, and maybe it's too late then. If you want to know the truth, this is the only time to do it."

Something in my stomach fluttered, and I crossed my arms over my stomach to try to stop it from happening again.

When we got to the vegetable stand, I picked up three yellow peppers for Ma. Sally and Shankar had already gone on ahead to the little store with the candy and fruit preserves. By the time Raj and I got there, they were already eating.

"How'd you get that? You don't have any money," I said.

"Mr. Harper said we could have it. I told him that you were coming with the money. He knows I'm good for it, right, Mr. Harper?"

The gray-haired man behind the metal curtain smiled and nodded. "Three dollars," he said.

I paid him for what Sally and Shankar were eating, and bought some *tambran* balls for Raj and me as well. On the way back, Shankar found an old soccer ball at the side of the road in some bushes. He kicked it out, and he and Raj began to play a little game in the street as we went along.

"I'm pretty good at that," I said.

"Oh, yeah?"

"I used to be on a girls' soccer team. I'm a natural."

Raj kicked the ball to me, and I showed off some of my skills.

"Nice," he said.

We passed the ball in a circle as we walked, trying not to let it go rolling down the hill. Shankar was pretty good too. Only Sally struggled to move the ball where she wanted it to go. We were able to keep it up until we got to the flattish strip of road in front of Ma's house. I ran inside and handed her the peppers, then came back out to continue playing. Raj had set up four stones, two each on opposite sides of the street, to be the goals. He was the first one to score. Haysley was standing with his front paws on the top of the gate, and he barked to cheer us on.

"No fair," I said. "You rigged the goals so you would score. There's no cheating in soccer!"

He laughed. "It's called *f-o-o-t*-ball," he said. "Only Americans call it soccer. You guys need to join the rest of the world."

"We already have football."

"I don't know why you call that football. The ball hardly ever touches the player's feet. You should call that 'holdball.'"

I laughed. "Whatever. You're just jealous." I dribbled past him. "And pathetic."

"What? No way. You got cricket? I bet you don't even know how to play."

I shook my head.

"All right, Shankar. We have to teach these tourists how to play cricket."

Shankar jumped up and down, and then ran inside the house behind his brother. They came out with a cricket bat that looked like a slab of rectangular wood with a little handle, and a bunch of sticks. Raj set up the sticks and told us that they were the wickets, and that we had to make sure the bowler, the one throwing the ball, didn't knock them down. Sally and I looked at each other and laughed. Baseball was way better than this. But after half an hour of running back and forth between wickets, and dodging the large cork ball that Raj kept hurling at us, we decided that this was fun, though it was definitely a lot more dangerous than baseball. At least in baseball you had a mitt to catch the ball. In cricket you had to catch it with your bare hands.

Hours later we were sore from running, and the palms of our hands were red from catching and throwing the hard cork ball. Sally looked at her watch and pointed at it. It was time to make the phone call. Shankar and Raj put away the cricket equipment, and Sally and I invited them over for something to drink. As if on cue, Ma appeared on the porch with a tray that had a jug filled with freshly made passion fruit juice, and four glasses.

"Thanks, Ma."

"Thanks, Mrs. Charles."

We gulped down the whole jug in minutes, and sat on the

chairs, licking the sweet juice off our lips, with sweat still running down our faces.

"Okay. You're ready?" Sally asked. "Are you going to call, or am I?"

"I'll call," I said.

Sally held out the phone book for me to see the number. I picked up the receiver and dialed.

"Hello, Mrs. Jarvis? . . . Can I speak to your mother please? . . . Hello, hi. I'm Grace, Christine Brewster's daughter. . . . I mean Charles, Christine Charles. You remember her? . . . Yes, she, you went to school together. . . . Yes, Steven. He's my father." I looked at Raj and Sally and shrugged nervously. They waved me on. "I have a sister, too. Sally." I returned Sally's grin. "Yes, everyone's fine. . . . No, no, they're not here. We're staying with our grandmother. . . . Yes, she's fine too. . . . Oh yeah, we love it. We're having a good time." Sally gave me a hurry-up look, and I got to the point. "We want to invite you to a party. It's my parents' anniversary next month, and they're going to be here then. . . . A beach party . . . Great. We also wanted to have all their other old friends surprise them, but we don't know where to find them all. . . . Well, we want it to be a surprise, so we can't really ask them. Could you help us? . . . Yes?" I gave Raj and Sally a thumbs-up. "We have a picture with a bunch of you guys in it. I could show it to you. It might help you remember everybody. . . . Great . . . Thanks."

Mrs. Jarvis gave me the address at her job, and she told me to meet her there around lunchtime the next day. When I got off the phone, Sally did a little victory dance around the porch.

Raj leaned in close to me and whispered, "This time tomorrow you could know who your father is."

Even though the fluttering in my stomach had returned, and my heart was thumping loudly against my rib cage, I couldn't help but smile. I was beginning to feel like a detective, as experienced as Sherlock Holmes and as adventuresome as Harriet the Spy.

Seven

Mrs. Jarvis worked in Port of Spain, or "town" as everyone called it. It was about an hour's drive away. Aunty Jackie worked in town, but she left for work too early in the morning to take us, so Ma reluctantly agreed to take us herself. I knew she still wasn't happy about all the party guests, so I tried to keep her out of it.

"I'm sure Raj knows how to get there, Ma. He could take us. You don't have to go," I said.

"Raj? You crazy? You think I letting you travel all the way to town with some boy? Your mother would let you do that?" I knew better than to answer. "Huh! I didn't think so."

The next day, after Ma cleaned up the breakfast dishes and set out what she wanted to make for dinner, she went to her room and closed the door. A half hour later she came out dressed in a blue flowered dress, stockings, black sandals, and an old black purse nearly the size of my school backpack. She fluffed the bright flowered cushions on the sofa and armchair and adjusted all the doilies and the porcelain figures that sat on top of them. Then Ma went to the door and began to jingle her keys in her hand as a signal to Sally and me that she was ready to go. We put on our sneakers and followed her out.

We walked to the taxi stand and stood in the hot sun for a long time while Ma tried to decide on a taxi and driver that she liked. There were green-striped maxis marked "PoS" that came and went, but she didn't even look in their direction. Just as Sally and I began to shift anxiously from one leg to the other and fan ourselves with our hands, a car pulled up in front of us.

"Good morning, Mrs. Charles. How you doing today?" the driver asked. He leaned out of the car window, exposing his bald brown head to the brutal sun. "It hot, eh?" he added, swiping a handkerchief over his shiny dome.

"Oh-ho is you, Mr. Roberts. Mornin', mornin'. You going to town?"

"I going where you tell me to go, Mrs. Charles." He looked at Sally and me. "Who these nice young ladies with you?"

"These are my grandchildren, Christine's girls."

"Nah man, you can't be old enough to have grandchildren."

Ma sucked her teeth and tried to suppress a smile. "You can talk a lot of nonsense, yes? Just take us into town." She ushered Sally and me into the car. "And try and get us there in one piece, please," she added sternly.

Sally and I exchanged looks of panic.

"Come man, Mrs. Charles, don't frighten these girls. You know I driving thirty years and you never hear me in no accident." He looked in the rearview mirror and smiled at Sal and me, trying to make us relax.

Once we were on the road, Sally and Mr. Roberts launched

into a conversation that lasted the whole forty-mile ride into town. As Sally leaned forward to hear better, Ma and I settled back against the hot vinyl seats. Ma smelled of the fried salt fish *accra* she had made for breakfast. I was beginning to feel hungry again, just thinking about it. Mr. Roberts wove out of crowded San Fernando and hit the open highway. On either side of the highway, the occasional unpainted wood house and grazing cow or goat appeared, but mostly there was grass that grew so long and thick that when the wind blew, it rippled like emerald-colored water. Mr. Roberts pointed out the few sights as we went along: a stadium named after a Trinidadian Olympian, a gorgeous mosque with a gleaming golden statue standing next to it, and a mall with amusement park rides. Sally wanted to go on the Ferris wheel, but Ma said no.

We arrived in Port of Spain in no time. The streets were crowded with people wearing bright colors that exaggerated the sun's heat. I wiped my forehead with the back of my hand and shaded my eyes. How could Ma wear stockings in this kind of weather? Mr. Roberts dropped us off at the taxi stand, and Ma counted out her money carefully and paid him. Then he disappeared into the waves of rippling heat rising off the asphalt.

Now the sun was beating directly on us. Ma opened up an umbrella and Sally and I huddled beneath it like we were in a downpour. Behind us was a small lighthouse that looked like it hadn't been used in years. Ahead of us, cars crisscrossed along streets with no lights and no stop signs. Ma set a fast pace and Sally and I quickstepped to keep up with her and the umbrella.

On every available spot along the sidewalks, there were vendors selling T-shirts, dresses, jeans, belts, and even shoes. In the few spaces between them were doorways to office buildings, more stores, and restaurants. But one crack in the wall of vendors looked like the entrance to an alleyway. Along the alley there appeared to be more vendors, but instead of the cheap clothes that were on the street, they had leather sandals, purses made of some kind of stiff round objects, and tiny bottles filled with yellow, orange, and brown liquid.

There was a heavy scent in the air around this alley, of something I couldn't quite put my finger on. I breathed in heavily. It was sweet and sharp. I hesitated, wanting to go in, but Ma rushed us past it and across another busy street.

We came to a large park with red metal railings all around, reaching tree height. Ma turned away from it and went down probably the quietest street in Port of Spain.

"Here we are," Ma announced. Sally and I looked at an old, but well-kept building in the middle of a block. We read the directory and found Mrs. Jarvis's office, as well as a hairdresser, a dentist, and a lawyer's office. "She's on the second floor." Ma snapped the umbrella shut and stowed it in her ample purse. We walked up two flights of stairs and Sally knocked on the door.

"Come in," a woman's voice called.

There were two women sitting in the room behind desks that were piled with books and stacks of old paper. The whole room smelled like a musty library. A dusty ceiling fan circled in the air overhead.

"Is that you, Mrs. Charles?" the woman closest to us said. "How you doing? I see age didn't touch you at all."

"Eh-eh, Sheila. I remember you now," Ma said, moving forward to pat her on the shoulder.

"You remember me? I used to be a whole lot smaller," Mrs. Jarvis said, smoothing her blouse down against her tummy.

"No, no, you didn't change at all," Ma said.

"And these are Christine's girls? I can't believe it!" she said, slapping her hands to her cheeks. "Look at how big! Lord, I can't believe it's been so long since I've seen Christine, yes?" She shook her head as she stared from Sally to me, and back again. "Look, Florrie," she said to the other woman in the room. "These big girls are one of my school friend's children. Can you believe it?"

"I believe it," the woman said. "Children grow like weeds. I couldn't believe that mine turned five the other day." She extended her hand, and Sally, Ma, and I shook it. "I'm Florence Wilson."

Ma settled into a wooden chair in front of Mrs. Jarvis's desk.

"Yes, sit, sit," Mrs. Jarvis said, pulling two more chairs over for Sally and me, and then settling into her own. "I can't believe how good you looking, Mrs. Charles."

"Well, these two will be here all summer to put some more gray in my head. So far they're doing a fine job of it too." The three women laughed.

"So how are your mummy and daddy doing?"

"Good," Sally said.

"They must be real Americans now, eh? With accent and everything."

Sally and I laughed and shook our heads. "They sound like you guys," Sally said.

"Right!" she said, clapping her hands. "That's good. You can take the Trini out of Trinidad—"

"But you can't make them talk like a Yankee!" Mrs. Wilson finished. The women laughed again, and this time Sally and I joined in.

"So you girls want to have a little party, eh?" Mrs. Jarvis asked.

"A beach party," Sally said. "At Maracas."

Mrs. Jarvis smiled. "So that's your favorite beach, eh? You stopped at the lookout?"

"It's high," Sally said, nodding. "We could see the whole beach below us, the ships out at sea, and the hills surrounding everything. It was really cool. We took loads of pictures. Grace said she'd throw me off the top."

Mrs. Jarvis laughed and winked at me. "I'm sure she wouldn't do that. Well, you don't have to ask me twice to come out to the beach. And it will be very nice to see Christine and Steven again after all this time. When did you say it was again?"

"In about four weeks," Sally said. "On a Saturday." She looked at a Chinese food take-out calendar they had tacked up on the wall. "The seventeenth."

"But we still need help finding our parents' friends," I said. I looked at Sally and raised my eyebrows.

"Oh, yeah!" Sally handed the pictures to Mrs. Jarvis. "Aunty

Jackie said that you might know where everyone was."

"Two of these fellas don't work too far from here. Bucky and Nimble." She turned a picture around to show us who she was talking about, but turned it back too quickly for me to get a good look.

"Aunty told us about Bucky," Sally said. "But which one is Nimble?"

Mrs. Jarvis pointed to the guy our aunt had called Jack.

"Oh, I get it," I said. I turned to Sally. "Get it? Jack be nimble?"

"Oh. Everybody has a nickname except me. Even Aunty Jackie calls Grace 'Red,'" Sally complained.

Mrs. Jarvis laughed. "You have such a pretty name, Sally. Why would you want anybody to call you something else?"

Sally instantly perked up and grinned. "Thank you, Mrs. Jarvis," she said. She looked at me smugly. Brat.

Mrs. Jarvis laughed out loud. "You hear that, Florrie? They want to call me Mrs. Jarvis. No, no, girls. You have to call me 'Aunty Sheila.' I know your mother too long for you to be calling me Mrs. anything."

"What about the other guy in the picture?" I asked. "You don't remember him?"

She looked at the pictures again. "Well, I can't even make out the face on this one. I'm guessing it's either Bucky or Nimble, or this other fella," she said, squinting at the other photo. "I didn't know him well at all. Bucky and your mother and I were friends first. The three of us lived near one another, so we used to travel to school together all the time. I only became friends with the others later on."

I took mental note of the new information. Bucky knew my mother the best. I guess that meant it could be him.

"Let me give these guys a call. I'm sure they could help you." Aunty Sheila leaned back in her chair and punched in the phone number with a number-two pencil.

I took a deep breath and sat straight up at the edge of my chair.

"You anxious to get your little party going, eh?" Mrs. Wilson said.

"Yep," Sally answered enthusiastically, swinging her legs back and forth under her chair. She hadn't even taken notice that Mrs. Wilson was talking to me.

"Yes, can I talk to Mr. Simeon or Mr. Bennet? Thank you." Mrs. Jarvis drummed her fingers on the desk as she waited. I shadowed her, and drummed my fingers on the arms of my chair as well. In moments my father could be on the other end of that phone call.

"Hi, Jack? Yes, how you doing? . . . I have some pretty young ladies here who want to invite you to a party." She winked at us and smiled. "I'm telling you!" she said into the receiver. "You remember Christine and Steven? Well, their girls are here on holiday, and they're planning a surprise party for their parents. Sweet, eh? . . . Yes, him too . . . Well, how about this, did you boys have lunch yet?" She held her hand over the receiver and whispered to Ma. "Did you all eat lunch?" Ma shook her head. "All right, hon, we'll meet you for lunch. . . . Sure, that's a good spot. We'll head over to you, and we'll all go from there, all right? . . . Right, well see you in a few minutes. Tell Bucky to loosen that girdle, eh?" she said with a chuckle. "Right, 'bye." She turned to us. "Okay, girls, we'll meet Jack and Bruce for lunch. I hope you're hungry."

All the muscles in my body tensed up. Either one of them could be my father. I wasn't sure if I was ready, but there was no turning back now.

Eight

In the steaming streets of Port of Spain, we pushed our way through people wiping their foreheads with handkerchiefs or carrying their shade under umbrellas. I wiped my hand over my face and tried to think of something smart and witty to say, something that would instantly identify me as someone's long-lost daughter. Something that would make him—my father—like me. It was too hot to think. Sally and our new aunty walked ahead and chatted about what we were going to do at the beach, and what kinds of food people should bring to eat. Everything came so easily for Sally. Ma and I walked quietly behind them under the umbrella.

"You all right, child?" Ma asked me.

"Uh-huh. It's just so hot."

"Mm-hmm." She pulled a small handkerchief with red and blue flowers from her bag and handed it to me to wipe my face.

"Thanks, Ma."

Aunty Sheila led us to a large gray building. We followed her up a flight of stairs and through a pair of glass doors to a receptionist at an old wooden desk. She asked her to let Jack Bennet or Bruce Simeon know that we were there. Ma lowered herself into a plastic chair, and Aunty Sheila sat in the only other available chair on the other side of the room. Sally and I leaned against the wall near Ma. My heart beat hard against my chest, and I looked down to see if anybody else could see it vibrating against my T-shirt.

"What are you doing, Grace?" Ma asked.

I jerked my head up. "Nothing, Ma."

A good-looking man came jogging into the room and stopped in front of Aunty Sheila. He was wearing a pale gray suit and a flowered tie. "How you doing, darlin'?" he asked.

"Hey, Jack. I'm doing good. You looking nice, man," she said, getting up to give him a little squeeze.

"Girl, I'm always looking nice," he said, smoothing down his shirt and passing a hand over his neat graying hair. His smile was warm and easy, and there were little wrinkles around the sides of his mouth and the corners of his eyes that deepened more as he smiled. I found myself smiling too. It's hard to look at someone who's smiling all the time and not smile yourself. He didn't look like the man in the picture, but it was hard to be sure. I wished I could see if he had the birthmark on his left shoulder. When he turned to look at Sally and me, my stomach did a little flip. I crossed my fingers behind my back. "And you must be Christine's daughters. They're just as beautiful as their mother, eh, Sheila? Look at these eyes," he said. He walked over to Sally and me and held our chins in both of his hands for a moment. "Just like Christine. Gorgeous." I tried to hide my blush, but there was nowhere for me to hide.

Sally giggled out loud. She was used to getting compliments on the way she looked. She never got embarrassed the way I did. Then he looked at Ma. "And you, young lady, what can I do for you?"

Ma looked up at him and arched an eyebrow. She set her mouth like she wanted to suck her teeth and tell him off, but she didn't. He grinned widely at her, and then she blushed a little bit too. "You too much, yes?" Ma said.

"I can't believe that's you, Mrs. Charles. You are looking too good. Tell me, what's your secret? We could bottle it and make a fortune. What do you say?"

Ma laughed out loud. Sally and I exchanged surprised looks. We had never heard her do that before. "You are no good, Jack. Trying to sweet-talk an old woman like me. You are no good."

Sally nudged me and grinned. I smiled back and crossed my fingers. A wish was forming in my mind, but I couldn't be sure, so I held my breath and kept it half formed at the tip of my tongue. If only I could take out the photographs and just ask him.

"Well, let me get Bruce and we'll be off."

He came back with a chubby man with unruly hair. He extended his hand as he came around the corner. How was I supposed to tell which of them was the one?

"Hello, Sheila. How you doing, girl? I haven't seen you in so long. You keeping well?" He pumped her hand up and down hard and looked at the rest of us over his glasses. His forehead was wrinkled in a little frown. He didn't wait for Aunty Sheila to answer. He turned on his heel and flashed a buck-toothed smile at Ma while he still continued to frown. Now I knew where he got his nickname. "Is that you for true, Mrs. Charles?" Ma smiled and nodded again, and Bruce went over to pat her on the shoulder. "So how you feeling these days, lady?"

"She's feeling fantastic!" Jack said. "Look at her. I know women half her age who look years older than she does." Ma just kept on grinning. Bucky pushed his glasses up on his nose and nodded in agreement.

I looked from one man to the other and studied them carefully. I couldn't see which of them had my birthmark, and I couldn't come out and ask them. I felt like my head would burst open.

The six of us went to a restaurant that had a glassed-in balcony overlooking the street below. We got a large booth, and Sally wedged herself in with Jack and Bruce. Ma, Aunty Sheila, and I sat on the opposite side.

"So how long Steven and Christine in New York now?" Bucky asked.

"More than thirteen years," Ma said, giving me a sideways glance. "A long time now."

"Time does fly quick, quick, yes?" Aunty Sheila said. "It was just the other day the lot of us were going to university."

Jack and Bucky told us some stories about when they were all in university. I barely listened. Instead I looked from one to the other and back again, examining their features carefully, and trying to figure out which of the two I resembled more. On every count, Jack was winning. He was really skinny just like me, and he wasn't tall. We had the same reddish-brown complexion, and he had one dimple in his left cheek. I had one in my right. There was something else, too, something about him made me feel comfortable right away, and I never felt comfortable around people I had just met. On the other hand, Bucky had only two things going for him: His hair was just as unruly as mine, and the constant frown on his forehead was like a shadow over all his emotions. It was like someone had ticked him off a long time ago, and he never got over it. Maybe if someone had taken my daughter away and I had never seen her, I would wear a constant frown too. None of these observations were nearly enough to make a match. And there was only one way to know for sure. I waited impatiently for Sally to bring up the pictures.

"So you girls hear how we Trinis like to party, so you want to see firsthand. I understand, I understand," Jack said, nodding to himself and smiling.

"Yeah, so I want to find all of our parents' friends and invite them. We have these old pictures. Mrs. Jarvis—I mean Aunty Sheila—said you could look at them and tell us who the other people are and where to find them," Sally said.

Jack cocked an eyebrow. "So it's 'Aunty Sheila' now, eh? Well just for that, you girls have to call me 'Uncle Jack.'" He slapped Bucky on the shoulder. "And this here is your uncle Bucky."

Bucky smiled a buck-toothed grin. "Bruce," he said. "Call me 'Uncle Bruce,' okay?"

"Okay," Sally agreed.

"So what pictures you have there?" Uncle Bruce asked.

I gave them to him.

He grunted. "You girls are being very thorough, aren't you?"

"Well, the plan is to have all of our parents' old friends there. We figured it would be fun to go to the same beach with the same people and all," I said.

"Old friends, eh? We not that old you know."

"We don't mean old that way, um, Uncle Jack," I started to explain.

He reached over and patted my hand. One eye clicked down in a wink. My heart just about stopped beating. "I'm just joking with you," he said. It was exactly the kind of thing a father might do with a daughter. It had to be him.

Uncle Jack looked closely at the photos. "Oh, Lord! I was ever so young?" he said, holding a picture up to show Aunty Sheila and Ma. "And see? That's a handsome face, right?" he added to Sally.

Sally shook her head vigorously. "You mean my dad? Sure. He's handsome." They all laughed. Sally beamed.

"Man, you remember this day? We planned from the night before that we were not going to class the next day. Your mother never liked to cut class, eh? But she would go if Steven and Sheila were going. And of course Jackie went anywhere Christine went. It was a good thing we *break biche* too, it was so hot that day, and the air was so humid, you could just open your mouth and drink it. Who could study on a day like that? So real early, before the sun came up, Bucky took his father's old van and drove the lot of us to Maracas." Uncle Jack paused.

Aunty Sheila continued the story. "Well, when we got there,

it was still early enough in the morning that we didn't see a soul on the beach. The vendors who set up on the lookout weren't even there yet."

"We got a nice secluded stretch of beach to ourselves. Clean, smooth sand, not a footprint in it yet. And the water was nice and blue, not yellow, like how it gets later in the day when everybody been kicking up the sand," Uncle Bruce said. He looked down at the picture Uncle Jack handed to him. It was the one that was all blurred. He squinted at it. "This isn't you, Jack?" Uncle Bruce said.

Every muscle in my body strained. My heart was beating so loudly I could barely hear.

He passed the picture to Uncle Jack. "Yeah, man, that's you hugging up on Christine and Sheila."

"Nah, nah, that isn't me. I think this is Steven, man."

"How do you know it's not you?" I blurted out, trying to control my voice.

He shook his head. "If you think I'm slim now, you should have seen how scrawny I was back then."

"Are you sure?" I asked.

"Of course," he said.

My heart sank. The wish I had been rolling around at the tip of my tongue crumbled, and I swallowed hard.

"Well, we weren't the only ones who went Maracas that day," Uncle Bruce said. "What about the footballer? I mean soccer player," he corrected himself with a nod to Sally and me. "Remember, he brought a ball and we played a match on the sand? Yes, man. Don't look at me like you don't know who I'm talking about. He used to play on a north team. What was his name? Mitch?" he asked Aunty Sheila and Uncle Jack.

"You mean Mitchell? I remember him. And he had a friend, a Venezuelan fella," Uncle Jack said. "What was his name again? Ricardo?"

"No, it wasn't that. It was something . . . religious," Uncle Bruce said. "Jésus! That's what it was. Jésus."

"Mitch and Jésus weren't really our friends," Aunty Sheila said. "I think your mother just felt bad for them because they were outsiders. The Venezuelan guy had just moved here, and Mitch was kind of quiet."

"Huh! Quiet is putting it mildly," Uncle Jack said. "Anyway, the Venezuelan wasn't there. Only Mitch is in the picture with all of us. This is him, right here."

"And what was his last name?"

"Mitchell was his last name. I don't remember his first name, though. We just called him Mitch." The others nodded their agreement. Mitchell. My father's name is Mitchell.

"Okay, so the guy in the picture with my mom and Aunty Sheila had to be Mitchell, right?" I asked quickly before the moment passed.

"It looks like," Uncle Jack said. "But don't worry about this picture. There's a much better one with him in it here." He took the picture and pretended that he was going to throw it out. "You should just get rid of this. You can't see anything in it."

"No!" I reached my hands out to rescue the picture from him. Everybody looked at me, including people at nearby tables.

"Grace!" Ma hissed.

"The picture belongs to Aunty Jackie. I can't throw it away."

"But there's no reason to yell," she said. "Children these days, eh, Jack?"

He nodded. "Don't worry. Mine carry on the same way."

"So how do we find Mr. Mitchell?" I asked, trying to sound as calm as I could.

"I think he living somewhere behind God's back, in the bush, like one of them crocus bag people."

Sally screwed her face up. "What are crocus bag people?"

"Crocus bags are what they pack rice into before it's sold. These crocus bag people are farmers. They live off the land, and they don't come off their little plot of earth except to sell at market. They like to wear clothes they make for themselves from whatever they have on hand. Sometimes you get a nice rice bag, and it doesn't have any rips. You cut here and there, make a few stitches, and voilà—instant shirt! Or you take two bags and make a pair of pants," Uncle Jack said, miming how they sew the bag together. He was pretty funny. Our group was laughing hard. Even people at nearby tables were looking over and snickering at his antics. All of them looked like such a fun group. I could just imagine what it must have been like to hang out with them when they were younger.

"So they farm rice?" Sally asked.

He laughed. "No, hon, it's just a nickname. And they don't really wear crocus bags either. At least not anymore."

"Most of them a little cracked in the head, though," Uncle Bruce said.

My stomach knotted up at the thought.

"You would have to be to go living in the bush like that," Aunty Sheila said.

"I don't trust none of them, nuh," Ma said.

"Well, do you know what his phone number is, so we can call him?" Sally asked.

They all laughed. "A phone!" Aunty Sheila said. "No, they don't have anything like that. No electricity, no radio, no car, and no phone."

Oh, great. Just my luck. "So how do we find him?" I added.

Aunty Sheila shrugged.

"But you don't know if he's really one of these crocus people, right?" I asked hopefully. "You said that you think he's living in the bush, so how do we find out for sure?"

"Is it really that important?" Ma asked. "You have three of their best friends right here. That isn't enough?"

"It won't be the same if everybody isn't there," Sally whined.

"All right, all right Sally," Aunty Sheila said soothingly. "Just relax."

"But Gracie's right. You're not sure. You could be wrong, and then my party won't be perfect."

Uncle Jack nodded. "Well, I know a guy who used to work in the oil fields with Mitch. That's how I heard he left the work all of a sudden to go and live up in the hills, growing plants and making clothes or something. I can ask my friend if he knows how to find him."

"Is there any other way we could find out?" I asked.

"I think you've found out enough," Ma said. "There's no need to go dragging some stranger out from the hills."

"Don't worry, girls. You have the best of the bunch right here. So when is this party again?" Uncle Jack said more brightly. "I have to make a batch of my famous *buss up shot*."

"Oh, Lord! Poison!" Aunty Sheila said, grinning.

"Well, if you making *buss up shot* roti," Uncle Bruce said, "I will have to make the curry goat to go with it."

"The party is next month on the seventeenth," Sally said.

Seeing my disappointment, Aunty Sheila leaned toward me and whispered, "Don't fret, baby, we'll see what I can find out about Mitchell for you, all right?"

I nodded. I stared out from the balcony at the street below. Right now, my father could be walking out on the street in the hot sun, or hidden in a hill somewhere wearing a rice bag made into pants. I slumped back in my seat. Even though Aunty Sheila and Uncle Jack offered to look for him, I knew that I was going to have to find him myself. He was my father. I needed to know who he was so I could know who I was. And I only had four weeks left to do it. After that I'd be back in Brooklyn, and I wouldn't have another chance. But without a first name, a phone number, or an address, how was I going to do it?

Nine

Days later neither Uncle Jack nor Aunty Sheila had come up with any new information about Mitch. I suspected that Ma's attitude might have discouraged them from looking harder. Sally complained that her plans were ruined. I tried to convince her that there was still a way we could find out about him. It was my last resort, and it was risky.

"We're going to have to ask them, Sal. You don't want the party to be ruined because everybody in the pictures doesn't show up, do you?"

"How can we? Mom always figures out what we're doing when we start snooping. If we ask them, she's going to know something's up, and she'll get it out of us. She's good at that."

"So we'll just ask Dad."

"Oh, like he won't tell Mom, or she won't hear him when we're on the phone?"

She had a point, but it was a chance I had to take if I wanted to find out where Mitch was. "Well, do you have any other ideas? I'd love to hear them," I said, folding my hands and tapping my foot.

Sally looked at the phone, then back at me, and sighed. She knew she was beaten.

"Right then, so when they call on Sunday, you'll ask Dad. I'll tell you exactly what to say."

"Me? Why do I have to ask? Why can't you ask? You have all the big ideas."

"Relax, Sal. You're not going to get in trouble. Besides, Dad never asks you to explain anything, but if I ask him, he'll want to know why I'm asking about all of that."

She raised her eyebrows. "True."

I didn't know if Sally was just agreeing that Dad always gave her what she wanted, no questions asked, or if she was agreeing that I always got questioned. Either way, my heart hurt from knowing that even my little sister had noticed that our father treated each of us differently.

"So you'll ask Dad?" I asked, making sure she wouldn't back out.

She nodded. "Yeah, okay."

Sally went into the living room and plopped down on Ma's couch to watch TV. She folded her legs under herself and arranged the flowered cushions around her. She watched intently as equally graceful girls in Indian costumes and wearing jingly gold jewelry on their wrists, ankles, and attached to their hair, ears, and nose did a traditional East Indian dance to the beat of the *tassa* drum. It was the Trini version of a talent show. But it had none of the high-tech logos, visual effects, or elaborate stage sets as the ones back home. I went outside and sat on the front steps. Haysley lumbered up and crawled into the space under my knees. He looked back at me and whimpered, begging for attention.

"Okay, Hays," I said, and began to stroke his filthy fur. "You need a serious bath, mister." He yawned and put his head down on the step.

I tried out my true name softly. "Grace Mitchell." I thought about the man in the photograph, and wondered why I hadn't seen the resemblance before. It was kind of hard to tell with just one picture, and he was a bit far off, but we clearly had the same smile, our shoulders sloped the same way, and of course there was the birthmark. Because he stood so far off in the group picture, it was hard to see the mark on his shoulder, but I was sure it was there.

The smell of ground meat cooked with peppers and plump raisins wafted out from Ma's kitchen. She was making *pastels*. They had come to be my favorite meal this summer. I could see her rolling out the cornmeal on the banana leaves and folding the meat inside. Last week she had folded them with foil, and I had been disappointed. I wished that all I had learned this summer was that you should always make *pastels* inside banana leaves.

"Hey! Hey!" Raj yelled from his yard.

I jumped, and the image of my father and me chatting amicably over a plate of Ma's *pastels* disappeared. Haysley picked his head up and whined because I had stopped stroking his fur.

"Hey," I called back.

"Your parents call yet?" he yelled again over the brick fence.

"No. Tomorrow."

He nodded. "Right. You told me that already."

I nodded back, and yanked a tick from Haysley's back, putting it on the concrete steps. He sniffed at it briefly, then flicked his tongue out and scooped it into his mouth.

"Ewww, Hays. That's really gross."

Haysley looked back at me and seemed to shrug. I fully expected him to say, "Well, he was eating me."

Raj came down his front steps and motioned for me to meet him at the fence. "So is Sally going to do it?" he asked in a soft voice.

I nodded. "Yeah. She knows our dad would never ask his sweet little Sally why she wants to know." I scraped at some moss on the bricks with the toe of my sneaker. "It's because she's the favorite."

"Shankar is the same way. I can't remember getting away with half the things he does. But we're boys. We still get away with more things than you girls."

"Must be nice."

"Yeah, but we don't get as much attention."

"What do you know about how much attention girls get?"

"This girl in school is always telling me how easy I have it because my father don't need to know where I am every minute. But I keep telling her that at least somebody care where she is." He wiped the hair away from his forehead.

"Your father cares where you are."

"Not my real father."

"Mine neither."

"You don't know that yet."

"Honestly, sometimes I wonder why I want to know at all."

"Not all of them that live up in the hills are bad, you know. I mean some of them a little cracked in the head, yes, but most of them just want to be by themselves and live off the land. That not so bad, I think. Nothing and nobody to worry about, just build your own house, make your own food, bathe in the river when it get real hot. Sound kind of nice to me."

"That isn't what I was thinking about. It's just that if he knows I'm out there somewhere, how come he isn't trying to find me as hard as I'm trying to find him? And anyway, everybody seems to think that those crocus bag people are pretty unfriendly and dangerous. Ma especially. What do you think they're doing up in the hills? They could be doing anything, you know."

"You think I ever been up in them hills? I don't know what they have or don't have and I am not looking to find out, nuh."

"See, you think the same thing as everyone else."

"Well, I didn't say that exactly."

"No, but you're not looking to go up in those hills either, are you?"

Haysley pricked his ears up and made a little whimpering noise at me from his perch on the steps. I lowered my voice and my head a bit.

"Sorry. It's just that how would you like to suddenly find out that you have a father who everybody thinks has gone crazy, and is living in the hills, wearing clothes made out of produce bags." I sank down against the side of the wall. "Maybe he's insane. Maybe that's why he's never come looking for me."

"Well, how would you like to know your father used to drink away all your family money and beat on your mother every week."

"At least you always knew who your father was."

"You think that's better? Growing up with that every day? Sometimes I think, maybe one day when I'm older and I'm making my own money, I would go and find him. Then I could tell him I could give him enough money so he could stay in the rum shop all day and drink until he pass out. And he would look sad and glad at the same time, and then I could walk away and leave him sitting there, wondering if he should ask me for the money or if he should be ashamed of himself and just let me go my way."

His eyes narrowed and focused on something in the distance. The unruly lock of hair lay undisturbed over both eyebrows and cast a shadow over his eyes. Still, I could see that they were beginning to shine, the way eyes shine when they just start to get wet with tears.

"I guess you've been thinking up that plan for a while," I said, breaking his concentration. "But how will you know where to find him?"

"My mother said she would tell me if I ask her, but I can't ask her until I'm grown."

I wondered if my mother was waiting until I was older to tell me too. It was like Raj could read my mind.

"But she had to say that, eh? I already knew most of the story. It's better if you find out now," he said, jerking his head to the side to flick the hair out of his face. "You don't know that you'll get the chance to find him later on."

"It's what I'm going to find that scares me."

"Whatever you find will be better than not knowing."

"I don't know, Raj. What kind of person would not try and contact his own daughter for thirteen years?"

"So what am I going to say, then?" Sally called down from Ma's porch, cutting me off.

"Sally! Quit sneaking up on people, will you? And keep it down. You want Ma to hear you?" I leaped up the stairs to her side. Raj waved good-bye and headed back up the stairs to his own porch. I turned back to my sister. "You tell him that Ma took us out shopping in Port of Spain, and we met one of his friends. He'll ask you what the friend's name was, and you say you don't remember, and he'll run down the list of guys he knows, and we'll get it out of him that way."

"Oh," she said, nodding. "That's pretty good."

I reached up and tapped her on the head. "It's because I'm smarter than you."

"No, you're just older than me. You've had more time to learn how to be sneaky."

I shrugged. She had a point.

Overnight, among giggles and whispers, and holding our breath when we thought we heard the sound of Ma waking up, we came up with every possible question our father could ask, and I coached her all night on what she should say, and how she should say it to not sound suspicious. I told her that I figured she shouldn't say the name Mitchell, that he should guess it himself so that he wouldn't suspect that he was being baited for any specific information. I knew it meant that my mother might hear him say it, so I figured I'd send her to look for something in my room while Sally talked to Dad. We talked for so long that we nearly didn't sleep. It was like when we were younger and we used to sneak into each other's rooms at night after our curfew and sleep under the same covers.

Sal and I fell asleep happy, and when the phone rang on Sunday, it woke us. Both of us grabbed for the receiver, but I was faster. I flashed her a victory grin and answered.

"Hello? . . . Hi, Mom . . . Good . . . Yeah, we went into Port of Spain a couple of days ago. . . . Not much, just walking around and shopping and stuff. What are you guys up to? . . . Really? . . . Yeah, I'm having a good time. . . . No, I'm not mad. You're right, I can hang out with my friends in Brooklyn any summer. . . . I guess I was a little upset last time, but now it's more, um, interesting. . . . Hey, can you do me a favor? Sal and I have a bet about something. There's a book of poetry on my bookshelf, can you get it for me? I need you to read something. . . . Yep, that's the one. Thanks, Mom. I'll talk to Dad while you go look."

Dad and I chatted briefly, and then Sally got on the phone. She looked a little nervous, and I was afraid that she might blow it, so I tried to look positive whenever she looked in my direction.

"Yeah, we went to town with Ma," she told him. "Yeah, it was hot. I was sooo sweaty! . . . Uh-huh . . . We saw a friend of yours," she said, looking at me for support again. I nodded encouragement, and she continued. "I don't remember exactly. . . . He said he knew you from school. . . . Um, I dunno. Something with an *M*."

I gave her the thumbs-up. Excellent. Just like we rehearsed. Then it occurred to me that I should pick up the other line and listen in, just in case he gave us some useful information. But the other line was in Ma's room, and she didn't like us snooping around in there. I decided to chance it. I gave Sally the "keep going" signal and grabbed the notepad and pen that was on the table at the side of the phone. Ma was in the kitchen hovering over a pot, so I eased past her and tiptoed into her room at the back of the house. I picked up the phone gently, squeezing my eyes nearly closed, as if that would help to minimize the sound, and put the receiver to my ear. My father was talking.

"And he said he knew me from school?"

"Mmm-hmm," Sally said. She was beginning to sound nervous.

"Did he have dreadlocks?"

"Uh, I don't remember."

"You'd remember something like that, Sally."

My heart sank. Maybe I shouldn't have left her in the room alone.

"He was wearing a hat," she said. "Hard to tell."

"Kind of hard to hide a whole lot of dreadlocks under a hat, Sally."

"Well, maybe he cut them off. I don't know."

"Okay, sweetie. Ah, was his name Mitchell?"

My heart skipped a beat. *Come on, Sal*, I thought. *Don't overdo it.*

"I think so," she said slowly. "Sounds like it."

"Karven Mitchell?" he asked. His voice sounded strained.

"Yeah, yeah. Karven. I remember it was weird. I mean, it's not exactly a name, is it?" she said.

"Well, it suits him. He's kind of a weird guy."

"But you were friends anyway, right?"

"No, we weren't. He went to the same school as your mother and I, but I didn't care for him, or his friends either, really. Your mother knew him a little better. He's not the friendly type like you are, babe. He liked to be alone most of the time. Somebody told me that he went up in the hills to live a few years back. It figures," he said, grunting. "You can't trust people who go up in the hills to live. So I don't know what he was doing in town, unless he was dropping off his stuff to sell."

"What stuff?"

"I hear he makes leather goods—handmade shoes and bags and belts. Stuff like that. They sell them in the Drag Mall on Frederick Street. Was it there that you saw him? Did your grandmother take you there?"

"You mean that place with all the incense? Yeah, we met him when we passed by there, but we didn't go inside."

"Well, it's a good thing you didn't. That's not so safe a place to go. And I don't want you going there under any circumstances, do you understand?"

"Okay, okay. So do you know if we can find him anywhere else?"

"What do you want to find this guy for? I told you, he lives up in the hills. You have to watch people like that. And he was never very . . . normal."

We hadn't rehearsed anything like this, and I knew Sally wouldn't know what to say. I put the phone back gently and snuck back out of Ma's room as quickly as I could. Ma looked as though she was going to walk out of the kitchen just as I got out of the door to her room, but she stopped and walked over to the refrigerator instead. She opened the door and reached down. For the second time I was able to slip past her undetected. I motioned for Sally to give me the phone, and plopped down in the chair.

"Hi, Daddy."

"Grace, I don't want you girls talking to strangers in the street, you hear me?"

"I know, Dad."

"I can't believe your grandmother let you talk to someone like Mitchell. Maybe I should talk to her."

"Well, she's not here," I said, lowering my voice.

"What do you mean, she's not there?"

"She needed to get something from the store. She was going to send me, but I was waiting to talk to you, so she went herself," I said.

"All right, well, watch out for Sally, please. She thinks she can just go up and talk to anybody who says 'hello' in the street."

"Sure, Dad."

When we finally got off the phone with our parents, Sally and I shared a worried glance. Neither of us was prepared for Dad to be so angry. I felt stupid. I should have seen this coming. If he had gotten so angry when I told Sally the story of my birthmark, why wouldn't he be angry that Sally and I might have actually met my father? I wondered if he and Mom would argue again the way they had the night Sally sprained her wrist. I didn't think it was possible for Dad and me to have a worse relationship. But even from a thousand miles away, I was making that happen. And it was possible that I was making a big deal out of nothing. I didn't know who the man with my birthmark was, really. He could have been anyone. It could even be a coincidence that our birthmarks looked the same. It was a very old, blurred photo. Maybe there wasn't even a birth-mark.

Doubts buzzed in my head like a swarm of angry bees. But as distracting as they were, the question of why I always felt so different had lodged itself firmly at the back of my mind. I accepted that I might have another father so easily because instinctively I always knew that I belonged somewhere else. I knew I had to keep searching.

Ten

"Now what?" Sally asked me. "Everybody thinks this guy is a weirdo, and Dad doesn't even like him."

I felt desperate. There had to be a way to find out more about him. I had to keep going, and I had to convince Sally to go along with me. "You weren't listening. He wasn't friends with Dad, but he was Mom's friend, so he still has to come. Besides, if he makes belts and handbags, he's probably not a weirdo. He's probably just . . . creative."

"Yeah, right." Sally picked up the little guest list she had written up and started to cross him off. I grabbed it from her.

"Wait a minute. If he sells the stuff he makes in that mall in Port of Spain, then somebody there would know him, and they will be able to tell us if he's a weirdo or not, or at least tell us where we can find him."

"You think we should still go there after what Dad said?"

"Why not?"

"Because Dad said it was dangerous. He said not 'under any circumstances.'"

"I told you, Sally. Just because Dad says something is one

way, doesn't mean he's right. Not always."

She got off the couch and stared down at me angrily. "All of a sudden, it's either your way, or Dad's way. Well, you know what? I pick Dad's way. The weirdo's off the list." She crossed him off so hard that the page ripped in her hand.

"Who cares about you or your stupid list?" I said, standing to face her eye to eye. "I can find Mitch without you."

"What's going on out here?" Ma was standing in the doorway of the kitchen with a towel gripped tightly in one fist. Sally took one look at the worried expression pasted on my face and opened her mouth.

"Shut up, Sal," I said under my breath.

"Why?" she asked, shooting an angry look at me.

Ma shifted from one foot to the other. "Somebody better start talking soon, you hear? Or crapaud smoke both yuh pipe."

"Huh?" Sally asked.

Ma raised her eyebrows and gave us a stern look. Well, we knew what that meant.

"We asked Dad about Mitch, Ma," she said.

"No, Sal!" I hissed.

She gave me a sideways glance and kept on talking. "We told Dad that we ran into a friend of his, and we tried to get him to tell us where Mitch lived. But Dad got pretty mad, so we didn't get much out of him."

Several seconds passed before Ma responded. "I see. So you tried to trick your father into giving you information. It's not enough that you already lying to him about this party, eh?"

"Well, it was mostly Grace's idea." She looked over at me

and smirked. I couldn't believe it. I wanted to hit her.

"And how you know this Mitchell want anybody to find him? The man move out to the hills for a reason, you know. He not looking for two nosy little children to come finding him just so he can go to some party. But the two of you ain't think about that. No, all you think about is yourselves." She shook her head at us. "I don't know how you get selfish so. Well, at least your father put a stop to this stupidness. Now you can't bother that poor man, eh? And that's final."

Ma looked directly at me. I didn't know what to do, but I knew enough not to turn away when she was looking at me like that.

"Don't make up your face like that, Miss Grace. You are older. You supposed to be showing your sister what to do and what not to do, but no, you are the one instigating all the trouble. What you have to say for yourself?" I offered nothing. "I see. I guess all that can come out of your mouth are lies and ways to manipulate your parents. But you won't be manipulating me, missy. I not as easy as your parents."

"And Ma, I only went along with it so that I could get all of Mom and Dad's friends here for the party. I thought it was important," Sally said.

Ma turned toward her, both hands on her hips, and flame coming out of her eyes. "So important that you will meddle in grown people's business? So important that you will go looking for a man that don't want to be found? You didn't find some of your parents' friends already?"

Sally nodded.

"And that's not good enough for you?"

Sally dropped her eyes to the floor and tried to hold back tears. "But Grace—"

"But Grace nothing," Ma interrupted her. "You don't think for one minute that anybody would believe Grace got you to do something you really didn't want to do, do you? Tread carefully, you two. I have my eye on you." Ma turned on her heels and went back to the kitchen. Even the floorboards creaked angrily beneath her step. As soon as she was gone, Sally started to tear up. She walked into the bedroom, and I followed.

"You got me in trouble," she said.

"I got you in trouble? You ratted me out! If you had just kept your mouth shut, Ma never would have known. We would still be able to find Mitch and everything would've been fine."

"Are you still on that? Don't you get how angry Dad was? And exactly how would we get back to Port of Spain without Ma?"

"I had a plan for that."

"You were going to lie again and sneak out?"

"Well, what would you do?"

"Port of Spain is far. We couldn't get there by ourselves."

"Well, I can."

"You're still going to go? After what Ma just said? Are you crazy? What if she finds out? Then what?" She shook her head slowly. "We're already in trouble." A fresh batch of tears ran down her face. "And she'll definitely tell Mom and Dad."

"She won't."

"How do you know? Even if she doesn't tell them now, when

TRACEY BAPTISTE

she finds you sneaking all the way to town, she will then. And then the surprise will be ruined, and we'll get grounded, or worse."

"Fine. I'll do it all by myself then."

"So now she don't want to go and find him?" Raj asked as we sat by the side of the street after lunch.

"She won't do anything that might make Dad mad at her."

"Nah, man. She can be pretty brazen if she wants to. I think your grandmother just scared her."

"Believe me, Raj, it's mostly because she's afraid she won't be everybody's favorite if she's caught. We're better off without her."

"Well, maybe she has a point. If your grandmother finds out that you sneaking off to town, she going to be plenty mad."

"What are you saying? You think I should drop it? You were the one who said that this was probably my only chance to find out about my father, and that if I didn't do it now, I'd probably never find out. Ma's not going to help me, Sally won't come along, and now you think I should just forget it?"

"Hey, take it easy. That's not what I said. I don't think you should drop it. You should definitely find out. I just think that maybe there's another way."

"There's no other way, Raj. So are you going to help me or not?" I looked back at the house, and the windows to Sally's and my bedroom. "Little Miss Perfect can stay at home and bawl in Ma's apron if she wants. I need to find him."

"Look, just because you find out you have some other family,

94

doesn't mean you should treat the ones you already have badly."

I felt ashamed, but I wouldn't show it.

"All I'm saying is maybe you should talk to your sister about it. That's all."

I shook my head. I couldn't explain this to Sally without telling her why I really wanted to find Mitchell. I felt guilty that I had dragged her into this mess. She was right. It was my fault that she had gotten into trouble. My heart beat louder as fear bubbled up inside me again. Everything had become so confusing, but I couldn't turn back now. I knew too much to just stop looking for the answers to my questions. I had to be strong. "Forget it," I said to Raj. "We're on our own."

The next day I told Ma that Raj was going to show me around San Fernando, and that maybe I would do some shopping for my friends on High Street. She wanted us to take Sally along, but Sally said that she had a stomachache and wanted to lie down. Ma made us promise that we wouldn't get into a maxi-taxi. Raj said that we would walk so we'd see more stuff, but really it was so we'd have an excuse for being out for a long time.

As soon as we cleared the hill and were hidden from the house, we ran to the taxi stand and boarded a green-striped maxi-taxi headed for town.

"If I die in this maxi, Ma will raise me from the dead to kill me," I said to Raj.

"Me too."

We didn't have to worry about that, though. We got into

town in record time, amazingly unscathed. We paid the driver and stepped out onto the hot concrete with wobbly legs.

"Maybe we should take a regular taxi back," I said.

"Can't," Raj said. "They cost too much money."

We went straight to the Drag Mall. I was ready to question everybody we saw in there. As we stepped inside, the Drag Mall suddenly seemed far more dangerous than I remembered. It was dark and damp, and the cracks in the tin ceiling allowed shafts of sunlight to beam down on tiny rivulets of dirty water at the center of each alleyway. The metal gates that closed up each store at night were partly rusted, and the paint was flaking off. I heard my dad's voice in my head. "Keep a sharp eye and ear out, Grace. Don't let anyone take advantage of you." It was the same advice I had grown up with. He started telling it to me on the soccer field, and then when I started walking to school by myself. With my senses alert, I strode confidently up to the first stall. There were the hard round bags that I had seen before. They were actually scooped-out calabash gourds that someone had cleaned and carved and painted. The tiny bottles of yellow, orange, and brown liquid were different scented oils. And along with the oils and the incense, there was the strong sweet smell that I remembered from the first time we passed by. A man wearing a large knit hat that covered most of his long gray dreadlocked hair was using a pole to hang handbags on a hook above his head. He turned and caught me staring.

"What can I help you with, Princess?" he asked with a warm smile.

"Hi. I'm looking for a Mr. Karven Mitchell? He makes belts

and bags and stuff, and drops them off to be sold somewhere in here."

"Lots of people sell belts and handbags around here, Princess. I don't know anybody named Mitchell, but you can ask around." He gestured to the maze of dim paths around us. "I hope you find who you're looking for." He bowed his head slightly, and we knew that was our signal to leave. I didn't even get a chance to show him my pictures.

"Thanks," we said.

Raj and I went to every little store that sold leather goods with our pictures, but no one was able to help us. On the way back out, we passed the man with the gray dreadlocks again.

"Princess," he called as we passed by. "You know, a lot of people who come here to sell have found religion."

I looked at Raj. If we were in for a religious lecture, I was going to bolt. Raj looked back at me with the same scared look that I imagined was on my own face.

The old Rastafarian laughed at the two of us. "Don't look so afraid. What I'm trying to tell you is that the people here who find religion have to be reborn. And you know what happens when you're born?"

My eyes darted back to Raj. He looked as confused as I did. "No," I said.

"You're cold and naked?" Raj offered.

The old man smiled. "Well, that's true, but it wasn't what I was thinking of. I meant that you have to be named." He waited for Raj and me to catch on, but when we didn't, he continued. "Most of the people here aren't called by the names they were given as babies. When they found religion, they became new people with new names, and whole new lives. Understand?"

I nodded.

"I see you have pictures. Can I have a look?"

"I'm looking for this man. His name is, well, maybe it used to be Karven Mitchell."

"These are old pictures. And this one's not very good, is it?"

"They're more than thirteen years old," Raj said.

I shot him a look, and he shrugged in apology.

"Maybe I can help you," the man said. "Come back in half an hour. Then we'll see."

"You mean you think you know who this is? And you think that he'll be here?"

"Maybe it's who I think it is, and maybe it isn't. Like I said, these pictures are old." He bowed his head. "Half hour."

"Okay, thank you, thank you."

"I didn't say it was for certain. A half hour."

"Right. Thanks."

I couldn't help but feel that finally I was getting somewhere. After all the leads and dead ends, I could finally meet my father. I looked at Raj and we grinned at each other. I was glad that Sally wasn't here. She couldn't know about this yet.

"Now he's right," Raj said. "It mightn't be Mitchell, you know."

"It's going to be, Raj. I just know it."

"You thought the same thing about the other guy, Bucky, or Jack, or whoever."

"Yeah, but that was just me guessing. Mitchell is the only

other person it could be. He's the last one in the picture. This is it."

Raj reached over and squeezed my hand. We both kept walking along the sidewalk holding hands without saying a word. I felt better that Raj was with me, and I wanted to tell him something about how much I appreciated his help. I wanted to say thanks. Instead, I said the first thing that came to mind.

"I'm starving."

"Okay, let's get something to eat then," he said. Raj let go of my hand, and I followed him up the street.

Eleven

Raj and I sat on a bench in Woodford Square. The painted metal railings rose high around us, piercing the blue sky with their carefully painted red tips. In one corner there were people selling used books beneath a white tent. And all around the square were stately buildings—the Red House where Parliament met, the town hall, a library, and a small cathedral. Except for the new library building, the others seemed like they had been looking down on this square for a hundred years. People were walking around leisurely on the stone paths, smiling at us as they went by, or chatting with friends. Near the center of the square, a crowd had gathered around one man standing on a wooden box. A spray-painted banner behind him read THE UNIVERSITY OF WOODFORD SQUARE. He was talking at the top of his lungs about how people couldn't rely on the news to tell them what they needed to know, that they had to go out and find the answers for themselves. I wished I could block everything out and sit in silence. I concentrated on eating the doubles that Raj had bought for us from a cart at the corner of the square. Even with the soda I was drinking, my mouth felt dry. The fried dough and curried chickpeas from my doubles stuck in my throat. This was the longest half hour of my life.

I thought about my creative father, how he chose to go up into the hills to concentrate on his art. I knew he couldn't be the crazy rice bag–wearing hermit that everyone was making him out to be. He was an artist like me. Like those people whose art goes up in price after they're dead, even though nobody appreciated them while they were alive. That was why he had to live in the hills. Nobody appreciated him. I imagined my father brooding creatively over a piece of leather, surrounded by the deep green foliage of an untouched forest. I could hardly wait to meet him—Karven Mitchell, Designer. I knew he would be so amazing.

"You ready?" Raj asked, looking up from his watch.

Suddenly I didn't feel so ready. "I guess so."

"You don't have anything to worry about. This is what you wanted to find out, right?" He waited for me to nod. "Okay, so let's go."

He put a hand on my shoulder and steered me back to the stall where the old Rastafarian with the gray dreadlocks was waiting for us. Leaning on the old man's counter was a younger man wearing a white shirt that came to his knees, a pair of old jeans, and leather sandals. He had long dreadlocks too, but they were a glossy black, and he had them tied back into a neat ponytail.

"These are the two I was telling you about," the old man said as we walked up.

"Yes, I see," the younger man said.

I tried to smile, but couldn't. I wondered if I was really looking at my father. He didn't look much like me, but I crossed my fingers behind my back anyway.

The old man introduced us. "Children, this is Brother John. He might be able to help you."

I put my hand out to shake his. As he took it, I recognized that same sweet, sharp smell again. It was on him, and on the bag that was draped across his shoulder. It was the smell of new leather.

"Hi, I'm Grace," I said.

"My name is Rajindra."

"Hello, Grace and Rajindra. What are you doing in town all by yourselves?"

"We're looking for someone."

"How old are you?"

"Thirteen."

"Fourteen."

"I see, and your parents let you hang around in town all by yourselves? And I know you're not from around here," he said, pointing to me. "So you can't know your way around too well."

"No, I'm not, but we're not here alone," I said. "My grandmother isn't far from here, doing some shopping. We're going to meet up with her afterward."

He looked at both of us calmly for a few seconds, and then nodded. "So what can I do for you?"

I pulled the pictures out of my bag. "We're looking for this man. His name is Karven Mitchell." I glanced at the old man behind the counter. "At least, his name *was* Karven Mitchell. He might have changed it to something else." The younger man took the pictures from me. "I know that they're old pictures, but I don't have any better ones."

He nodded again.

"You think you know him, mister?" Raj asked.

"You can call me Brother John."

"You think you know him, Brother John?" he asked again.

"I do. What do you want with him?"

I looked at the old man, and he moved away to the back of the stall and began to rifle through a box.

"It's personal. I'd rather tell him myself."

"Well, he's a very private person. Why don't you tell me the story?"

Raj piped up. "It's her parents' anniversary. She wants to invite all of her parents' friends to a party for them."

"Who are your parents?"

"Christine and Steven Brewster."

He nodded, still looking down at the pictures. "You're going to a lot of trouble for a party, not so?"

I glanced at Raj. He gave me an encouraging look. "Well, it's a little bit more than that." I pointed to the other picture showing the man with the blurry face, then I moved the strap of my shirt over to show my birthmark. "We have the same birthmark," I said. "I want to know why we have the same birthmark." I looked at his shoulder as if a hard stare would bore through his shirt.

Brother John looked where I was staring, and then straight at me. It was like he was trying to read something in my face. I stayed still for as long as I could, but eventually I had to move.

"Does your grandmother know that you're out here trying to find this person?"

Raj shrugged. "Sure, she knows."

"Okay, then you come back with your grandmother, and I'll tell you what you want to know about this man."

"Well, it's going to be a while."

"I can wait," he said to me.

I looked at Raj. His mouth hung open. This was my only chance to find my father, and we were blowing it.

"You don't understand," I said. "My grandmother can't know what I'm doing. If she finds out, she'll tell my parents, and I can't let them know either. I have to do this by myself. I don't want to have to lie to anybody, but I won't find out . . . what I need to know if I tell them what I'm doing." My face had gone hot, and sweat beaded up around my temples. "You have to help me. Please?"

His eyes softened. "I can help you. But first I think you should talk to your family about why you're looking for this man."

"So you're not going to tell me where to find him?"

Brother John looked at me and sighed. Then he shook his head for a while. "You found him already."

I frowned. "You're Karven Mitchell?" I asked.

"People used to call me that, yes."

"Why didn't you say that all the time?" Raj asked.

"You didn't ask me that."

"Jeez an' ages!" Raj slapped himself on the head, and then shoved me on the shoulder.

I wiped the sweat from my face with the back of my hand and scraped my fingers through my hair. "You don't have red hair."

"No, I don't."

"Does someone in your family have red hair?"

He shrugged. "It's possible."

"You're the person I've been looking for."

"No, Grace, I'm not."

"Yes, you are. You just said that you were Karven Mitchell." I pointed at the picture of everyone on the beach again. "This is you, isn't it?"

"Yes."

"Well then, you're—"

"Not who you're looking for."

"What about the birthmark? We have the same birthmark!"

Raj touched my arm. I had been yelling. The people around us had stopped what they were doing to stare at the three of us. Even the old Rastafarian behind the counter was looking at me, like I was the weirdo.

"Calm down, Grace. I promise you, I am not the person you're looking for. You need to talk to your mother and father. But if you need me, you can always find me here. Every Tuesday and Thursday I drop off my things to sell. Okay?"

I was confused. If he was the last unidentified man in that picture, then he had to be my father, didn't he? So why wouldn't he say so? I felt like the tide was pulling me out to sea, and there was nothing I could do but let it. Before I could say another word, Brother John said good-bye to his friend behind the counter and began to walk out the alleyway into the bright city. The shirt that hid my proof billowed behind him in the tropical air. As he got to the entrance of the mall, he turned back to look at me. With the bright city behind him, I couldn't see his face very well, but his voice was clear. "I will see you again, Grace," he assured me. And with a nod, he was gone.

Raj pushed me gently out of the mall. He stood in front of me for a while, waiting for me to spout my anger, but I didn't. He leaned closer and I put my head on his shoulder. We stood on the sidewalk leaning against each other. People passed by and watched us, but we didn't care. Eventually we pulled apart, and Raj held my hand to guide me home. I was glad I wasn't going through this alone. I was glad Raj was there. It felt good to be with a friend.

Twelve

"So what you think you going to do?" Raj asked as we walked back to our houses from the San Fernando maxi-taxi stand.

"I don't know. I figured it would go better. Not like that."

"You thought he would just say, 'Hi, I'm your father, nice to meet you'? I told you it wasn't going to be easy."

"You know saying that doesn't make me feel any better."

I dragged my sneaker through the gravel at the side of the road and listened to it grate satisfyingly under my feet. We were at the top of the hill, and Raj's and Ma's houses were just below us.

"Do you think she'll suspect something?"

Raj looked at his watch. "We've been gone almost four hours. She'll probably think we should've been back long time. Don't worry. We have our excuse, and we'll stick to it."

I looked at the white plastic bag in my hands, filled with trinkets for my friends. We had picked them up at a souvenir shop near the Port of Spain taxi stand. "Ma has a way of knowing when you're lying, though. I don't know if I'm going to get away with this."

"Well, wasn't it worth it?" He saw the look on my face. "Well, at least you know what he look like now."

"He didn't even admit he was really my father. He just kept saying I should talk to my parents. But it's my parents not talking to me that got me here in the first place. This is their secret, not mine. And anyway, he is one of my parents."

"Just because he's your father, doesn't make him your parent. Harry isn't my father, but he's my parent. You know what I mean?"

"Parent, father, whatever. The fact is, I met my father today, and he didn't even care enough to admit that to me, his own daughter."

Shankar jumped out in front of us from a nearby bush. "Boo!" he screamed, and then erupted into laughter. "Come on, Sally! Come on! You missed scaring them with me."

Sally walked out from behind the bush. Her face had a look of shock and confusion on it. She looked like she did when I told her she might never meet her guardian angel.

"Oh no, Sal."

Her eyes wavered, and she blinked a few times to hold back the tears that had begun to gleam in them. There was nothing I could say.

Shankar tugged at her hand. "Don't cry, Sally. We can scare them again. Look, we'll go back in the bush and wait for them again, okay, Sally? Okay?" Shankar tried to pull her back into their hiding spot, but she yanked her arm away from him and went running into Ma's house. He ran after her for a few steps, then stopped and began to sob himself.

Raj sighed heavily, and then he looked at me. "Later, all right?" He waited for my nod. "Let's go, Shanky boy, let's go." The two of them walked away hand in hand.

"You bring something for me, Raji?" Shankar asked between snuffles. Raj pulled a mint out of his pocket and handed it to his little brother.

Shankar looked up at him and smiled. "Thank you, Raji."

If only it were so easy for Sally and me. From the very beginning we'd always been so different. Suddenly I felt all alone. Raj knew where he belonged. There was no question where Sally belonged. Only I had a father who didn't even want to admit that I belonged to him. But I had to put my hurt aside and deal with Sally. When I got inside, Ma was putting plates out on the table for dinner.

"You must be hungry by now," she said.

"Hi, Ma."

"You hungry or not?"

I nodded.

"You find everything you went looking for?"

"Yes, Ma. I think so."

"Good. This came for you." Ma pointed to a letter on the dining table. "And tell your sister it's time to eat. Your Aunty Jackie coming over for dinner. She called just now to let me know that she was on her way already."

Ma was back in the kitchen by the time she finished talking. I stepped quietly into the bedroom and found Sally curled up in a ball on her bed, with her back to the door. She was sobbing and sniffling. I put my letter from Maciré on the nightstand for later.

"Don't do that, Sal. Blow your nose." I got a pack of tissues from the dresser and tried to hand them to her. When she wouldn't turn around to take them from me, I put the box on the bed in front of her face. Then I sat on the edge of my bed, facing her back. We sat in silence for a few seconds, then she slapped the box of tissues off the bed. I went around and picked them up, and returned to the edge of my bed. I held the box in my lap.

"What did you hear, Sal?"

She sniffed a couple of times, but said nothing.

"You know Aunty Jackie is going to be here soon. You're going to have to show your face then." I waited a little bit, then I gave up and poured the contents of my bag out on the bed. I lined up all my little trinkets, little stick-figure sculptures of people playing steel pan, lying on beach towels, climbing coconut trees. All of them were on little stands that read TRINIDAD AND TOBAGO in red, white, and black lettering, the colors of the Trinidad and Tobago flag. I counted them and assigned one to each of my friends. Then I looked at the letter. Maci wasn't going to believe any of this. I wondered how I could even tell her. Would she think it was weird, now that my family was—different? A couple of our friends had parents who were divorced, but I didn't think that any of them had a family secret like this. Maybe I wouldn't tell any of them after all.

I opened the envelope.

Dear Gracie,

Girl, you are confusing! Either you like it there or you don't. And I want to hear more about the boy next door. You won't believe it, but our next-door neighbors moved out, and the people who moved in have a daughter who's our age. Her name's Alyssa Simone. She's so cool. Her older brother is really cute too. I'm heading over there now.

I can't wait until you get back home! Miss you!

Love,

Maci

P.S. The cartoon of you under the coconut tree made me laugh out loud! I wish I could draw like that.

If Maci's idea of shocking news was getting new neighbors, she might faint if I told her about my father. Maybe if I told her, she would choose her cool new friend over me. Maybe family secrets like this were meant to stay secret. Maybe that's why no one had ever told me. But she was my best friend. I was going to have to tell her.

Dear Maci,

I'm going to tell you the most incredible thing ever. You can't tell ANYONE. Don't even repeat it aloud to yourself. And you'll have to tear this letter up after you read it so no one will ever see it. Promise!!!

I found out that my dad isn't my real dad. My real dad is here in Trinidad, and I'm trying to get to know him. Raj has been helping me to figure this all out. He's really great about listening to me, especially

when I'm upset or feeling scared. But I really wish
you were here with me too. Things are so weird right
now.

Please don't act suspicious if you see my parents.
They don't know that I know.
Love,
Gracie

I looked up when the driveway gates clanged open, and a car crunched the gravel in Ma's driveway. Sally had fallen asleep. I put the letters and my souvenirs away and went outside.

As usual Haysley was trying to jump up and get his front paws on Aunty.

"Look, dog. Stop, nuh?" Haysley fell to all fours and trotted behind her. As she got to the front porch, she squeezed me against her side and took me into the house with her. "Mummy, when last you feed that dog?"

"He get feed last night, and he'll get feed tonight again. What's the problem?"

"That dog, every time I come here, he jumping up on me with his mouth open like I'm prime steak. It's like he ain't seen food in weeks."

"Look at the size of that dog, Jackie. He could stand to skip a meal or two and he'd still be fine." Ma looked Aunty up and down and opened her mouth to say something else, but turned back into the kitchen instead.

Aunty pulled her stomach in a little and fixed her blouse. "He not that fat," she mumbled to herself. "So how you doing, young lady? I hear you went shopping today? How'd that go?"

I nodded. "Okay. I got some stuff for my friends."

"Nice. But nothing for me?"

Should I have bought something for her? Maybe if I had bought something for Sally, she would talk to me.

"Oh, don't look so frighten', honey. Your aunty just making joke with you. Relax." She looked around the room for Sally. "Where little Steven?"

"The child have stomachache whole day, yes?" Ma said. "I thought she was feeling better and she went outside to play with the dog and the little boy from next door, but she just now come back inside and go to lie down." Ma started to put out plates of food on the table. She looked up at me. "What your parents usually give you children for stomachache? I think I'm going to have to boil some orange peel and make tea, yes? Your mother ever give you orange peel tea? I don't want Steven to say I wreck he child." Ma went back into the kitchen and pulled out long curls of dried orange peel that were hanging from the handle of a cupboard. It looked like she had been saving them for years. "We'll try it and we'll see," she said.

A grin started to spread across my face. Sally was going to hate having to drink that down. And then I remembered that she was mad at me.

"What you looking so for?" Aunty Jackie asked. "You not the one who have to drink that." Then she whispered. "And good thing, too. It taste real bad. Your grandma don't like to put sugar in nothing, so she going to have to take it bitter." She made a face, but I didn't laugh. "You all right, Red? You don't look too good yourself."

Ma looked out of the kitchen at me. "You not feeling good either? Well I better make some more."

"No, no. I'm okay."

"Well, you don't look okay. Better safe than sorry."

Aunty Jackie and I plopped down on the couch. She pulled me close and rocked back and forth a little.

Just then Sally came out into the living room. Her eyes were a little red and puffy.

"Oh, baby, come here," Aunty Jackie said, holding out her other arm. Sally crumbled into her and curled up on her lap. She shot me another angry look, so I wriggled out of Aunty's hold and moved to the armchair.

Ma brought out the orange peel tea, and made the two of us drink it down. We both made faces before the first sip, but it didn't taste too bad. It was pretty sweet, actually.

"I put honey in it," Ma said. "I don't want you to tell your parents I try to poison you," she said.

"What? You never used to put honey in it for Christine and me!" Aunty Jackie protested.

"Well, the two of you are my children. I can poison you if I want." Ma turned back into the kitchen to hide the smile that had sprung up on her lips.

I tried to get Sally's attention to see if she had seen Ma's face too, but she wouldn't look at me.

Dinner was quiet. No matter how many stories Aunty Jackie told, I couldn't bring myself to laugh at them, and Sally wouldn't look up from her plate. After dinner Ma sent Sally and I out on the porch with little bowls of soursop ice cream that she had spent the afternoon making. We only got a scoop each, because Ma said that she didn't know what was making us sick, and she didn't want to make it any worse. Aunty followed us out, sipping on bay leaf tea sweetened with honey.

The sun had just set. The navy sky on the east was slowly creeping toward the west, pushing the orange color down into the horizon. I thought of the sky as a giant ribbon sewn at both ends with colors that blended into one another, dawn into day, and twilight into night. I imagined that one set of stars was a gymnast who was holding the ribbon on a thin pole, twirling it constantly around the globe. I smiled at my own story, and tried to save it in my memory for the next time Sally and I were talking. She couldn't stay mad at me forever.

"You know," Aunty said, "one time there was this boy I had liked. Richard Henry." She chuckled low to herself. "He was a lot older than me. Four years. He was in the choir with your mother. Every Wednesday I used to have to go to meet Christine at choir practice at the boys' school. And every Wednesday, when all of them came out, I used to sit tall on a bench near the music room and try to catch his eye." She looked at Sally and me, waiting for a response. Sally stared down at the soggy remnants in her ice-cream bowl, and I looked back out over the railing at the stars that appeared as pinpricks in the steadily darkening sky.

"Well, this one day, Richard and your mother come out together. They were laughing, and he put his hand on her arm.

He didn't leave it there, he just put his hand on her arm for a second, and then put it back in his pocket. Your mother didn't even flinch. She just kept on walking, like it was nothing. Man, I was mad. He didn't even see me there, and I used to come there every week. I was so vex my face turned red! So when your mother come up to me, I just suck my teeth at her and walk away. She had to walk behind me the whole way home.

"Christine knew I liked Richard. So when we got home, she told me that she didn't ask him to put his hand on her arm like that. He just did it. She told me that she didn't like him at all, but it didn't matter to me one bit, nuh. As far as I was concerned, he liked her, and she had to do something to make it so. So it was all her fault.

"The next week I had a little plan to make him notice me. So when Christine rushed out before everybody else, I had to pretend that I had to tie my shoelace so he would have time to come out. As soon as he did, he looked around for Christine and walked right over toward us. I thought maybe he was finally coming to say hello to me. I stood up, between him and my sister, and said hello. He just stood there staring at me. My heart was beating so fast, girls. I thought everybody could hear it. Then I said, 'I like you Richard.'

"Well, he didn't know what to say, and the older children from the choir started to snicker behind their hands. I thought I was going to drop dead right there in front of everybody. Then he said, 'I didn't come to talk to you.' Well, that put everybody over. One set of laughing bust out all over the place. I didn't know what to do except run, but I couldn't even find the stairs, I was so confused. Then I heard Christine say, 'You can't talk to my sister like that. Who you think you are?' And then everybody said, 'Ooh,' all together, like something bad happened."

Aunty looked up to find both of us watching her eagerly, waiting for the end of the story. She smiled and took a slow sip of her tea.

"Well, what happened?" Sally asked.

"I turned around to see what was going on, and there was Richard holding his nose. I looked closer, and I noticed that he was bleeding. Your mother had punched Richard right in his face. Everybody was laughing. Your mother just walked right over to me and said, 'Nobody treats my little sister like that. Let's go,' and we left.

"Richard quit the choir because all the boys were laughing at him, and all the girls thought he was rude." She chuckled. "Bet he was never rude to anybody's sister again." She looked at the both of us. "It didn't matter what we were fighting about. Christine and I always stuck together. She was always there for me, and I was always there for her. Nothing came between us. Well, not for long, anyway."

I looked at Sally. She had been looking at me, too, but her eyes darted quickly to the floor.

"What if it's a big something?" Sally asked.

"Nothing's bigger than how much you and your sister love each other," Aunty said. She picked up all the bowls and spoons and headed for the kitchen.

Sally and I stayed quiet for a while. Haysley groaned and

whined at a few mosquitoes. Out on the main road a few cars honked their horns.

"I think she made that whole thing up," I said.

Sally nodded. "Yeah, it was kind of lame, right?"

"Seriously. If I wanted to watch an after-school special, I would've turned on the TV."

Sally laughed, but kept looking at the floor. "How do you know for sure about . . . about what you and Raj were talking about?"

I took a deep breath. I got the pictures and handed them to her. "Look, Sal. Look closely." I pointed to the man's shoulder.

Sally rolled her eyes and folded her arms. "I hate your stupid birthmark."

"I'm not a big fan of it myself. I wish I could just rub it off."

"So what's the big deal?"

"Two people don't just happen to have the same birthmark."

She thought for a while. "He could be some long-lost cousin."

"Don't you think that Mom or Aunty Jackie would know that? They were all friends."

"He wasn't a friend of Dad's."

"And that's the other thing. Dad got so angry when I told you the angel story. He made me stop talking about it. And he got so angry when we told him that we ran into Mitch. He practically banned us from going there. It's like he's trying to keep me away from something. He knows, Sally. He knows he isn't my real father."

"So you went to find Mitch?"

"Yes, but he won't admit he's my father."

"Good. So now you can just drop it. Right?"

I shook my head. "No, Sal, and keep it down. I don't want them to find out what I'm doing. I don't even know if they know about this." I looked inside to see if Ma and Aunty Jackie showed signs of hearing us, but they were leaning against the kitchen counter chatting. I turned back to Sally and kept my voice low. "What would you do? If you knew your father was out there, wouldn't you want to find out about him?"

"No."

"You're just saying that because you don't want me to. You have no idea what this feels like." I looked out into the warm starlit night. "Well, it doesn't matter if you understand or not. I'm going back. I have to."

Thirteen

I got my chance a week later, when Ma decided to go to the hairdresser. I wondered why she had decided to go now, when she hadn't gotten her hair done all summer, but I figured maybe she wanted to look nice for when my parents came. It was a Tuesday, perfect timing for me to go back and talk to Brother John. Before she left that morning, Ma made lunch for Sally and me and told us how to heat it up on the stove. Ma didn't believe in microwave ovens. She grabbed her big black purse and went to the door.

"All right you two, be careful, eh? Mrs. Seepersad right there if you need anything." She looked at us and took a final glance around the house, as though she were making note of where everything was before she left us in her house alone. "Right. I gone."

Sally went back into the bedroom and threw herself on the bed. But her bad mood did not sway me. I felt like I was going to burst open. I sat nervously and stared at the clock, waiting out the long ten minutes I figured Ma would need to find the right taxi to take her to the hairdresser. As soon as the time was up,

I went to the porch and gave Raj the signal. He went ahead to make sure that Ma wasn't waiting in any of the taxis at the stand. I tossed on my shoes and waited at the top of the hill. When Raj signaled that all was clear, we jumped into the first maxi-taxi headed for Port of Spain.

I sat stiffly on the cracked seat as we rode into town. My mind was filled with what I might say to Brother John, and what he might say to me. I guess I must have looked really worried, because somewhere between the mosque with the gold statue and the exit of the highway, Raj leaned over to me and patted my shoulder. "She'll be okay," he said. "Don't worry yourself."

I looked at him and smiled. I felt a little guilty that while I was busy thinking about my father, it was Raj who was concerned about my sister's feelings. I wondered what she was doing all alone in the house, but as I did, the maxi stopped at the Port of Spain maxi-taxi stand.

Raj and I ran straight to the Drag Mall and found the Rastafarian vendor who had helped us the week before.

"We've come to see Brother John."

He looked calmly at the two of us. "He came by every day last week. He's never come by so often to see me. But I don't think it was me he wanted to see." He winked at me.

I knew what that meant. I smiled back. "Do you think he's going to come today?"

"Oh, he was here already."

"Where is he? You mean he's gone?"

"You just missed him, but don't worry, if you come back

tomorrow, I'm sure he'll be here again."

"I can't come back tomorrow," I said. "This is my only chance."

"How long ago did he leave?" Raj asked.

"Not even five minutes."

That was long enough. It only took two minutes to get from the taxi stand to here.

"Which way did he go?" I asked.

The man pointed out to the street. "I didn't see which direction he turned, though."

"All right, thanks." I turned to Raj. "Let's go."

We ran out of the mall. "If we just missed him, he couldn't have gone very far," I said. "I'll go left, and you go right."

We jogged in different directions, looking in every storefront for Brother John. One street over, at a health food shop, I found Brother John sitting on a stool, sipping a drink from a plastic cup.

"Hello," I said, panting. "I've been looking for you."

He put the cup down. "And I've been waiting for you. So, did you talk to your parents?"

"No, but I don't need to. I only need to talk to you because—" I stopped to catch my breath.

"Because what?"

"Because I am talking to my parent." Everything slowed down as I waited for him to say something. Even the busy street outside hushed to hear what he was going to say.

"I told you. I'm not who you think I am," he said.

I was prepared for this. "Show me your birthmark," I said.

"Ah, yes, the birthmark."

"Show it to me," I said. "The one just below your left shoulder."

"So that was how you figured it all out," Brother John said. He unbuttoned the top of the long shirt and showed me his left shoulder. I stepped closer for a better look. There was nothing there. No angel hand. Not even a slight discoloration. As I stared baffled at Brother John's unmarked shoulder, Raj ran into the store.

"Let me see the other side," I said.

Brother John pulled his shirt over to show his other shoulder, but there was nothing there, either. He wasn't who I was looking for. I felt sick and weak. I reached out and leaned on one of the stools at the counter. I had come to the end of the road.

"I don't understand," I said. "I really thought that you were my father."

"Did you really think so, Grace?" he asked.

I rubbed my temples. What was I missing? I stared out into the street. A group of people walked past the shop. They were wearing brand-new Trinidad and Tobago T-shirts, and had red-white-and-black handkerchiefs tied around their heads and necks. Tourists. I watched as they asked a woman passing by their group to take a picture of them, then they all smiled for a group shot. They thanked the lady, took their camera, and kept on going.

"The group picture," I said to no one in particular. "If you were the only people on the beach that morning, then not everybody could be *in* the picture because someone had to *take* the picture. So who took the picture?" I turned to look at Raj and Brother John. "Uncle Bruce said there was a student from Venezuela." I looked right at Brother John. "And he was a friend of yours. You played soccer together. And he's my father."

"That's right, Grace."

"So where can I find him?"

"That's not for me to tell. Now that you've figured it out, you should call your mother and ask her to tell you."

"Please," I said. "You can tell me right now. I've waited so long trying to figure it out myself. All I know is that he's Venezuelan, and his name is Jésus." I took a deep breath. "Oh no, is he in Venezuela?"

Brother John shook his head. "He isn't in Venezuela, and his name isn't Jésus, either. Your father's name was Angél Rodriguez. He really loved your mother."

"What do you mean 'was'?"

"This is why I thought you should talk to your mother." He watched me carefully, as though he wasn't sure how to continue. "I'm sorry, but your father died a long time ago, Grace. He died before you were born."

"How? That's not even possible," I blurted out.

"It is. He died in a car accident about six months before you were born."

"What happened?"

"He was in a maxi-taxi. It was speeding down the highway one rainy night, and the driver skidded on the wet road. I'm sorry, Grace. You shouldn't have to find out this way."

Mom should have told me, I thought.

"I'm sure your mother was waiting for the right time to explain all of this to you," he said. "It can't be easy for you to understand."

"No, I don't understand. How can my father be dead? I just found out about him."

I saw Brother John exchange a look with Raj over my head. Raj put his hand on my shoulder, but I shook it off. The two of them let me sit in silence for a long time. When I was finally ready to speak again, Brother John looked down at me patiently.

"If you were friends, then you know all about him."

"We were best friends. I know a lot about Angél."

"Okay," I said. "I want to know what you know."

Brother John smiled. "You and Angél are very much alike, Grace. He was very determined too. There weren't many challenges he couldn't face. When he came to the university to study law, he was determined not to let the hours of study get to him. He joined the football team I was on, and he never missed a game. He was really good, too. He could play any position, but he liked to field the goal. He said it was the thinking position, because you can see the whole game and position yourself to defeat all your opponent's best efforts."

"Goalie is my favorite position too."

Brother John went on to tell me about how he and my father became friends after Brother John had been injured in a match, and my father took him to the hospital and stayed with him until he woke up, even though it meant missing a deadline for a law report. And how he was able to argue with the professor to get the deadline extended, and he passed the class anyway.

Too soon, Raj tapped me on the arm. He pointed to his watch. "It real late. We have to go. Now."

I panicked instantly. It would take us at least an hour to get back to San Fernando, and I wasn't sure that we would beat Ma back to the house.

"I'm sorry. I have to go. How will I get a chance to talk to you again?"

"You did mention a party. Am I still invited?"

"Yes! I forgot all about that." I gave him all the information and he promised he would make it. Then Raj and I ran out into the street.

At the corner just before the taxi stand, I bumped into a small woman with thick red hair coming around from the other side. She put both her hands on my shoulders to steady me.

"Are you okay?" she asked with a warm smile.

For a moment I felt calmed. "Yes," I said, smiling back.

She tossed some of her curly hair over her shoulder, showing deep dimples on either side of her face. "Good." I kept going, aware of the time, but couldn't help looking over my shoulder to find her as she walked away—until Raj grabbed me by the arm and pulled me across the street and into a crowded maxi.

I started to think about what Brother John had told me. I felt confused and angry all at once. I wondered what it must have been like for my mother to lose someone she loved. I wondered if Angél was my mother's first love and my dad was second place. I knew what it was to feel like a consolation prize. Maybe that's why I always felt like I took second place to Sally, Dad's real daughter. Maybe that was why he hated the angel story. Angél. I got it now.

When I got to the house, Ma was already home. Sally was sitting quietly in the armchair next to the telephone. She and I looked nervously at each other and braced ourselves for the punishment that was sure to come. Ma was still wearing the clothes she had put on that morning. And her hair didn't look much different than it had when she left the house.

"So you back, then?"

I couldn't answer.

"Well, I hope you didn't take any maxi-taxi."

Still, I said nothing.

"So tell me what you know."

I looked at Sally, and then back at Ma. "I know about my real father. I know his name is Angél, and that he's . . . he was Venezuelan. I know you don't like for us to ride in maxi-taxis because he died in an accident with a maxi-taxi before I was born." Out of the corner of my eye, I saw Sally's head jerk up. I kept my eyes trained on Ma. I didn't want to see Sally's face. I couldn't bear it if this news made her glad.

"Have a seat." She patted the sofa cushions, and then got up herself. She went into her bedroom for a moment and came back with a box made of flowery cardboard paper. She handed it to me. "I knew you would figure it out one day. I told your mother so. I promised her I wouldn't help you find out, but I didn't say I was going to stop you either." Before I could open the box, she put her hand on top of the lid. "But I didn't like your lying, Grace, or the sneaking around. Still, I suppose you wouldn't have found out any other way." She sighed. "I was real worried about you, Grace. As soon as I knew what you were up to, I got worried. It's a hard thing to find out your family's keeping secrets. It's even harder when you start keeping secrets of your own. These are the things that pull us apart. I think after you and your parents have a little talk, things will be better." Then she smiled at me. "You are more grown-up than I thought, Grace. Not a lot of people would be able to find out something like this and handle it calmly. I underestimated you. You make me real proud."

"Can you tell me anything about my father, Ma?"

She shook her head. "No, baby, this is not my story to tell. But your mother will be here soon enough." She began to move her hand from the box so that I could open it, but then she stopped again. "But I never, never ever want to see you in one of those maxi-taxi vans again. You hear me, child?"

I nodded.

Ma began to walk back to the kitchen. "I don't think your mother could handle that twice." She sighed. "I am going to take a nap, girls. Maybe tonight you want to go out and get something to eat from the place out the road. I don't want anything. I'm going to leave my purse on the counter there. You can take the boys next door with you. I already asked Mrs. Seepersad."

"Yes, Ma," Sally and I said. We looked at each other. How had she figured out what had been going on? I shook my head and chuckled. You couldn't put anything past Ma.

Sally joined me on the couch and I opened the box. On the inside, the flowered paper was brighter, unaffected by the sun and years of neglect. I found a small picture album. There were a few smooth rocks, some cracked seashells, and a ring that was shaped into a flower. There was a notch at the top of the ring that looked like a piece was missing, and two leaves sprouted out of the sides to form the band. There were also some letters that Angél had written to my mother. Around the edges of the paper were little sketches of the two of them.

"That's why you do it," Sally said. "He was a doodler too."

These were much better than doodles, though. On the back of one letter, there was a full-page sketch of our mother. Even in black-and-white she looked like she was blushing.

"This one's really good," I said, feeling proud of my father, and prouder that we had something in common.

In the album we found pictures of my mother and Angél Rodriguez. But on the last page, there was a picture of Angél standing alone. The sun was setting behind him, and it looked as though light was shooting out from behind his head. My heart leaped, and I closed my eyes. I remembered that my mother always said that when she looked at the angel, the light around him was so bright she had to squint to see his face. I knew then that my mother had taken this picture. It was exactly the guardian angel that she had described. A warm feeling cascaded over me. It was the feeling of belonging.

Fourteen

The warm smell of roti skins baking woke me one morning a week later and covered me like a warm blanket. I took a deep breath in and carried the smell with me under the covers. I felt the thud from Sally's feet when she jumped down from her bed, before climbing into mine. She snuggled next to me under the covers.

"Mom and Dad will be here soon. What are you going to say?"

I shrugged. "I'll think of something when they get here."

"You're going to tell them right away?"

"I'll probably wait until tonight. I can't jump them as soon as they get in from the airport. Anyway, I think I should talk to Mom alone first."

She nodded. "Good idea."

We held the blanket up over our heads with our hands and feet like a tent, and listened to Ma puttering around in the kitchen. It was like when we were really little and played "fortress" in bed on Sunday mornings.

"You think she'll be mad at you?"

"I think she might. I did sneak around a lot."

"Maybe she won't be so mad. I mean, it would be different if he was still . . ."

"Alive?"

"Yeah."

"I guess it would be."

"Well, I'm glad he's not."

"Don't say that, Sal."

"Well, I am. If he was still alive, everything would change. And I don't want anything to change."

"But things kind of have changed anyway." I thought about Mom's old memory box. It sat on top of the dresser, holding on to pieces of a puzzle that made up part of my history. I was desperate to know the rest of the story. Ma said that when Mom and Dad decided to get married, Mom gave the box to her to hold on to, "just in case." I guess she was thinking that one day I would want to know my father, and that this might help. Ma told me to keep it. She figured that it would be easier for me to tell my mother if I had the box to show her. I was kind of hoping that Ma would tell my mother for me, but Ma said that this was between my mother and me, and she had already interfered enough. I was on my own.

I slipped off the bed and took some paper out of my stationery box.

Dear Maci,
I was wrong about so many things! And I still have so many questions. Everything is already so different. It's like I've grown up all of a sudden, and the stuff

that used to bother me, just doesn't anymore. Like Sal. She's not as bad as she used to be. Maybe she's grown up a little too.

I haven't talked to my mom yet. Just thinking about it makes my stomach queasy. I think I get how hard it would have been for my parents to tell me what happened. Maybe I would be upset too, if I were Dad. Even though things will never be the same, I'm still glad I found out. I think it's better to know, even if that means we're not the perfect family.

I'll see you soon.

Your best friend (I hope)

Grace

Sally poked me in the ribs, trying to read my letter before I folded it up.

"You're my half sister," she said.

I reached over and tickled her until she teared up. "I'm your whole sister," I said. "And don't you forget it."

She laughed. "All right, all right, but turn your head the other way. You've got morning breath."

"You too!"

"Do not!"

Sally struggled to get out of my hold and knocked us both to the floor.

"Jesus, Lord! What the two of you doing in here? You don't think it's time to get in the bath and clean yourselves? The morning nearly done already, and your aunty will be back from the airport with your parents just now." Ma clapped her hands together. "Come on now, get up and make these beds, and take your baths." She walked off muttering something about "children these days not knowing how to behave like young ladies."

Sally and I giggled and got up.

"Who takes a bath anymore?" Sally said to the door.

"Old people," I said. "They're nostalgic for back when there was no indoor plumbing, and they had to lie in a tub of water that they hauled in from the river every morning."

Sally giggled.

We had enough time to eat a little something and clean up before Aunty Jackie got to the house with our parents. Sally darted out to the porch, leaving me with the rest of the dishes. I took my time finishing, and met my mother and father after they had unloaded their suitcases from the trunk of the car and were coming up the stairs. Sally was already hanging off Dad's neck, begging for a piggyback ride. She was probably never going to outgrow that.

"There's my other baby," Dad said as he struggled up the stairs. I met him halfway and planted a kiss on his sweaty cheek. He held a small bag out to me, and I took it, so that he could hold Sally under one arm. "What has your grandmother been feeding you two? You're huge!" He looked up and down at Sally. "No more lift up for you, Sasquatch."

"I'm not a Sasquatch," she said, faking upset.

"Look at those feet," he said. "Tell me you're not a Bigfoot. You better run out in the jungle and meet the rest of your yeti friends."

Mom and Aunty Jackie came up behind him. "Come here,

Gracie," Mom said. "You give Mummy a kiss." I reached over quickly and kissed her on the cheek and let her hug me. I stayed close with her arm wrapped around me so I wouldn't have to look her in the eye. "Did you give your grandmother any trouble?"

I shook my head. "No, Mom."

"You had a good time?"

I nodded.

My father and Aunty Jackie dragged the suitcases into Sally's and my room. Sally and I were bumped to the couch for the rest of our vacation. While Sally told them stories about all the places we had been to, and what new tricks she tried to teach Haysley, I helped Ma put the food out on the table. I listened carefully to what Sally was saying to make sure she didn't let anything slip.

"Since you being so helpful today, maybe you can put the food away and do the dishes after lunch so I can catch a little nap," Ma said.

"Sure, Ma," I said. There was a lot of food and a lot of people. Clearing the table and doing the dishes could buy me at least an hour. I took a sideways glance at my mother as she laughed at one of Sally's stories. I tried to plot how I could stretch the afternoon out so that I wouldn't have to talk to her until tonight.

Ma called everyone to the table. She said grace, and we all settled down for lunch. Just as I was beginning to relax, Dad asked about our trip into town with Ma.

"I was surprised you took the girls anywhere near that Drag Mall," he said to Ma. "I didn't think you would want to be anywhere near there. What were you three doing in town?"

Mom looked worriedly at Dad.

Sally looked at me, at a loss for what to say. Ma continued to chew her food and didn't look up at anyone.

"Yeah, we did. We were sightseeing in town, and there he was," I said.

"Well, I'd especially like to know how you managed to strike up a conversation with someone from inside the Drag Mall. I know your grandmother wouldn't just let that happen," Dad said.

"Well, Brother John—Mr. Mitchell changed his name to Brother John—he was there when we were getting ready to buy something from the guy that he sells his stuff to. Anyway, we were buying some of his stuff and you know how Sally is, she just started talking to him and next thing you know, we found out that you used to be friends."

He frowned. "I thought Sally said you met him on the street."

"We did," Sally said. "He was walking to the Drag Mall, and we were walking in the same direction."

"You just said you were buying stuff," Mom said.

"And on the phone you told me you never went inside there, Sally," Dad said.

Sally and I bounced panicked looks across the table to each other.

"Well, somebody better start talking," Mom said, looking nervously from Sally to Ma and then to me.

The fear from Sally's eyes seeped into me like a fog. I went cold and numb. Any moment now, Ma was going to lose her patience with our lying right at her table, and tell the whole story to our parents. Then Aunty Jackie began to chuckle.

"Oh Lord, girls," she said. "You just as bad as your aunty. You can't keep secrets neither!"

My heart began to race.

"What secret is this?" Mom asked, concerned.

"Well, I suppose it's no harm now, right, girls? They going to find out by tomorrow anyway, eh? So you want to tell them, or should I just go ahead?"

Sally and I didn't budge.

"Oh, look at their faces. It's all right, girls. You couldn't keep that secret forever." She turned to our parents. "Well, they wanted it to be a surprise, eh? But your two lovely children went and tracked down a bunch of your old friends from school, and invited them to a beach party for your anniversary tomorrow. Nice, eh?"

"What friends? That Karven Mitchell or Brother John or whatever his name is, was never any friend of mine," Dad said.

Aunty Jackie shook her head. "Well, I guess you girls found him after. But I was talking about Bucky and Sheila and Jack."

"So you two went out looking for Mitchell?" Mom asked.

"We were just trying to get all your friends together," Sally said, attempting to sound innocent.

"Exactly," Aunty Jackie said.

"Daddy said maybe we could have a party, and I said that we should get all your friends together from in the pictures."

"What pictures?"

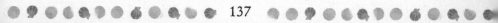

"From my old photo album," Aunty Jackie said. "Grace and Sally took out some old pictures and went around trying to find everybody in them to invite to the party. Show her the pictures, Red."

"Not now, Jackie," Ma said. "After we finish eating."

"So now this Mitchell is coming to our party?" Dad said.

"No," Sally said quickly. "We were just trying to get you to tell us where to find him. Uncle Jack said you all went to school together. But after I talked to you, I crossed him off the list." She went inside and got her list, which had been taped back together. Mitchell was clearly crossed off.

I kept my eyes on my full plate of food. I worried about how much this omission would cost me.

Sally's answer seemed to satisfy our dad. "Well, that's all right then. So what beach we going to?"

"Maracas," Sally said.

Dad clapped his hands together. "Ah yes, I haven't taken a dip in Maracas in I don't know how long. I can hardly wait. But I know we not getting there in Jackie's car alone."

"We'll have two cars," Aunty said. "The next-door neighbors are coming too."

Sally kept the conversation on the party, which let me off the hook. I sat quietly and ate very slowly. I cleaned off the table when everyone moved over to the living room to chat, and to see what my parents had brought from New York as gifts for Ma and Aunty Jackie. I went into the kitchen and strained my ears to hear what they were saying as I did the dishes. Any mention of the pictures again, and I was going to run down the back steps and over the fence. Maybe Mrs. Seepersad would hide me for a while until I figured out what my opening line was going to be to my mother. I was still staring out the window, looking for the best place to jump the fence, when Mom came in to see how I was doing.

"You're very quiet."

"I'm just doing the dishes."

She nodded. "I'm not sure if you're helping or hiding."

"Grace, where are those pictures?" Aunty Jackie called from the living room.

"I don't remember," I called back.

"Oh all right, I'll look for them in your room."

I spun around to stop her and dripped soapy water on the kitchen floor.

"Grace! What's going on?" Mom said.

I turned back to the sink and grabbed a dishtowel to wipe my hands on.

"No, Aunty, I'll get it for you," I said, but she was already in our room. I ran out to the living room. Aunty Jackie came out with the pictures, and my mother's memory box. My heart began to race. My mother followed me out from the kitchen. When she saw the box, she stopped and looked at Dad. Then she looked at me. I guess I wouldn't need to find an opening line after all.

Fifteen

"You remember this thing, Christine?" Aunty asked. "You used to put all kinds of things in here." She looked at Sally and me. "She never wanted me to see what was inside. I guess you don't mind now, eh, Chris?" She waited for my mother to give her the go ahead, and then she opened the box. She took out the little photo album and flipped through it. "You always used to keep your things in good condition, eh? No wonder you didn't want me touching them. How come I never see these pictures before? I know why, not a single picture of me. Who is this? Not Steven. Maybe that's why she didn't want anybody to see it, eh?" Aunty said to us with a wink.

My father did not respond. He looked up at my mother where she stood frozen. Aunty Jackie handed the album to my mother and began to examine the rocks and shells at the bottom of the box. My mother looked at the album and brushed imaginary dust off the cover. She held it gently without opening it.

"Good Lord, what you have all these rocks and pieces of garbage doing in here, girl? Oh, look. These are the pictures that the girls used to find your old liming partners."

Daddy looked at the second picture. He frowned and looked at it hard. Then he looked at Mom. "This you, Chris?"

She looked at the picture and nodded.

"I didn't remember this one. I guess it's the same as those in there." He lifted his chin toward the album in her hand. "I didn't know you still kept all this stuff."

"I didn't. I left them here with Mom," she said, looking at Ma.

"Well, I'm a little tired," Ma said. She got up and stretched a little. "I definitely need to take that nap now, before I start to get the food ready for tomorrow. You all will excuse me, eh?"

Aunty Jackie looked at her watch. "Oh Lord, I better go. I will see you all tomorrow. I hope your swimsuits are at the top of the suitcase so you don't have to dig!" She gave Mom a squeeze on the arm, and then gathered her beat-up purse and car keys and headed out the door. "I'll be here at eight o'clock to pick you all up, eh? So be ready to get moving."

"All right, Jackie," Ma said. "We'll see you in the morning then."

Sally and I followed her out and waved good-bye to her from the porch. When Sally turned around to go inside, I held her arm.

"What?"

"Maybe we should wait a little bit," I said.

"What for?"

"Just wait a minute." I looked back just in time to see my parents standing in front of the couch. Mom was still holding the little album, looking up at Dad with a frown. It wasn't an angry frown, but one that registered real pain. She kept rubbing her hand against her arm. Her mouth was open, ready to respond to whatever Dad was saying to her, but she never spoke a word. After a few seconds my father walked into the bedroom, and with a slight glance at Sally and me on the porch, Mom went in after him.

The two of us could hear our parents talking through the wood walls, but we couldn't make out what they were saying. We decided to go in and wait in the living room. Sooner or later one of them was going to come out, and I was going to have to explain what I knew and how I had found out. Mom's memory box still lay open on the coffee table in front of the couch. I looked at it, but didn't want to touch it.

"Do you think we're going to get in trouble?"

"I don't think you're going to get in trouble, Sal. But I'm pretty sure I will."

"Okay, good." She flipped through a book on the coffee table. "What do you think Mom's going to do?"

"That's not for you to worry about, Sally," Mom said.

Sally and I looked up and saw her standing near the arm of the couch. "Why don't you go help your father find his swim trunks?"

"Sure," Sally agreed. As she rounded the corner to the bedroom, she looked back at me. She looked scared. I tried to muster a reassuring smile, but by the time I did, she had already disappeared behind the wall.

Mom sat down next to me and dropped her hands in her lap.

"You okay, Grace?"

I shrugged. "Yeah, I guess so."

She turned toward me and put her hand on my shoulder. "Talk to me, hon."

I told her about the pictures, how I noticed the birthmark, and how I used Sally's idea as my cover. I told her about tricking Dad to get the information, and how angry Ma had been, and then how Raj and I went into town and found Mitchell, who had changed his name to Brother John.

She listened quietly and nodded. When I finished, she put her hands behind her head and relaxed back on the couch. "So that's how you figured it out."

"I wish I hadn't. This isn't fair. I mean, why did you do this?"

"Why did I do what, Grace?"

"With my father, I mean my real father. Why did you do that?"

"I didn't plan that, Grace. I didn't mean to do anything. Sometimes life throws you a little surprise. You just have to deal with it."

"So I was an accident."

"You were a surprise, but what a great surprise you turned out to be. I loved you. Your father loved you."

"Still, you and Dad lied to me. You should have told me."

"I'm sorry I didn't, but it's a hard subject to bring up, Grace."

"I guess so. I just wish—I just wish it wasn't true."

"I know it's hard to understand."

"Then why don't you explain it to me."

"What do you want to know?"

"I want to know what happened."

She took a deep breath and reached toward the box. She took out the photo album and opened to the first picture. "This was the first day I met your father. He came here on a scholarship to go to the university." Her fingertips ran along the edge of the plastic page. "He was funny and smart and talented, and really, really handsome." She laughed. "It wasn't hard to like him. He made friends very easily. Back then when your dad and I and all of our friends used to go to the beach, I would ask Angél to join us, but he was always too busy studying, playing soccer with Mitch, or drawing. That's where your artistic talent comes from, you know."

I smiled. "And he was a good soccer player too?"

"He was unbeatable. Anyway, one week he decided to come with us to the beach. That's when we took this picture." She fingered the one with my father's blurred face.

"How come it's so blurry?"

"We took it with an old Polaroid that Mitch had. The picture got splashed with sea water before it developed fully, so it never came out right. That's the only reason your Aunty Jackie had it, because you couldn't tell who it was. I kept all of the good pictures of Angél. I didn't have very much to remember him by, so I wanted to keep what little I had all to myself.

"Well, it wasn't much longer after that picture was taken that I found out I was having you. I was really nervous. I mean, we were young, but he wasn't scared at all. I'll never forget how happy he was. He laughed and said that we were going to have another little angel, someone who was going to be all the best parts of the two of us. He was sure you were going to be a girl. He was sure you were going to be beautiful." She stroked my face. "He was right."

Mom turned to another picture. "You have his eyes and his crooked smile. I loved his crooked smile. You have his wild red hair, too."

"I know."

She ruffled my hair a bit and pulled me closer. "It was really hard when he—after the accident. His mother came from Venezuela to take him back for the funeral. I was so sick from being pregnant with you that I couldn't even fly the twenty minutes it takes to get there. I never really got a chance to say good-bye. I tried to stay in touch. He had a sister, about the age Sally is now. But his mother was so angry about losing her only son, that she didn't want anyone in the family to have anything to do with his friends from Trinidad. She didn't even talk to Mitch at the funeral. It's hard to lose somebody you love, especially suddenly like that. You wonder why it happened to you, and you keep asking yourself what you could have done to prevent it. She probably thought that if she'd never let him go to the university here, then he would still be alive.

"So I was alone, and your dad always came by to see if I was okay, and if I needed anything. Whatever I needed, he got for me. It didn't matter how busy he was or how far away he had to go to get it. All of our friends thought that we were dating, but it wasn't that. We were best friends. So when he told me he was leaving to move to New York, I was really upset. I knew I would miss him a lot. I knew I loved him. I told him that I didn't want him to leave. So when he asked me to go with him, I said yes. We got married in a little church by the beach. And then we moved to Brooklyn."

"Did you love Dad the same?"

"Grace, I was lucky. A lot of people never find even one person they truly love, or one person who loves them back. In my life, I've had two."

"What about Sally and me?"

Mom pulled me close and smoothed my hair. "Okay, four. But you know what I mean."

I nodded and flashed her a smile.

"Are you okay now?" Mom asked me.

"I think so. But Mom, if I hadn't found out this summer, when were you going to tell me? Were you hoping I'd figure it out on my own?"

"Well, your grandmother always thought I should tell you before you figured it out. And she knew that you would find out on your own eventually if no one told you. She always said that it's the quiet ones you need to watch out for, because they see everything. She's a smart one, your grandma."

"Is there anything she doesn't know?"

"No, I don't think so."

"And what about Aunty Jackie?"

Mom took a deep breath. "Actually, she never knew. Like everybody else, she just assumed that your dad and I got married because of you. Only Mitch knew the truth because he and Angél were such close friends."

"You never told Aunty Jackie?"

She shook her head. "I never did. But I guess I can tell her now. No harm in her spilling the beans in front of you."

I laughed. "She really can't keep a secret, can she?"

"Nope."

We sat on the couch quietly for a while. I was enjoying the warmth from my mother's body and the way she smelled like fresh-cut flowers. Then I thought about how Sally, Dad, Mom, and I used to snuggle up together under one blanket when we went out to watch the Thanksgiving Day Parade balloons get pumped full of air the night before. We would stand there all snuggled together, passing a thermos of hot chocolate around until our toes got too cold, and we'd have to make a mad dash for the car. It had been a while since we all stood together close like that. I never realized how much I missed it until now.

"Mom, do you think Dad's mad at me?"

"Why would he be mad?"

"Because I'm not his real daughter."

"Even though he chose to be your dad, he never wanted to talk about your real father. Do you remember the night when you were nine, when you told Sally the story about your birthmark? Well, I think he was afraid that if you ever knew anything about Angél, the two of you would grow apart. He loves you, and he's afraid to lose you."

"I don't get it."

"Well, that night he saw you start to slip away from him. Now that you know everything, he thinks he could lose you."

"But that's not true!"

"But he doesn't know that, Grace. And you're the only one who can tell him. The two of you used to be so close. I think it really breaks his heart that you aren't anymore. I know he's sorry about that night. But fear blocks the love from coming through. Some people's hearts are paralyzed by fear. Don't you be one of them."

"How come you don't tell Dad any of this?"

"Sometimes you have to wait for just the right moment. It's like if you eat a fruit too early, it doesn't taste right, because it's green. If you wait too long, it rots on the branch. You have to get it at just the right time."

I let that thought rest for a while. I had so many questions about my father. Mom and I spent a long time going through the rocks and shells and all the things I thought were junk that lay inside the box. Some of the rocks were from the flowerbeds in the university. My father, Angél, had picked up one of them the day that he had met my mom. And every day that they met after that, he picked up another one. The bits of shells were from that day at the beach. We looked at all of the pictures in the album, and Mom talked for the first time about how much I reminded her of my real father—not just my hair, or my smile, but the way I got really quiet when I was thinking something over, or the way I drew all over every blank piece of paper I could get my hands on. We looked at the portrait of her my father had done, and she laughed through tears. She seemed relieved to be able to let everything out after all that time.

After we had gone through the box, Mom looked upset.

"What is it, Mom?"

"There was something else I kept in this box. It isn't here now. I hope it hasn't been lost."

I knew exactly what she was talking about. I fished around in my pocket and pulled out the flower ring. Mom smiled when she saw it.

"Ah!" She rubbed the notch at the top. "There was another piece to it. Angél used to wear it on a chain around his neck. He wanted the three of us to be a family. But it just wasn't meant to be."

"It's okay, Mom, don't cry."

"This can be your present from him." She gave the ring back to me, and I put it on my finger. "Sometimes I miss him like we just said good-bye yesterday."

I watched my mother shake the thought of that last good-bye, and that rainy night, from her mind. She wiped more tears from her eyes.

"Mom?"

"Yes, Grace?"

"I have one more question." She sat up and waited. "It's about the story you told me about my birthmark. Why'd you make it up?"

"What makes you think I made it up?"

"Well, it's not true, is it? An angel didn't put his hand on me and leave this mark."

"Yes, an angel did. Just not in the same way I told you. Your father didn't come down from heaven, but I had a dream about him that day, and he told me that he was fine, and that you would be too. Your father is that angel. So it is actually a true story."

"It's a good story, Mom. I've always liked it."

"Me too."

We sat together for a long time. She told me stories about my father in her gentle hushed voice, and the warm breeze coming through Ma's house blew her stories outside for the leaves to whisper. It was lovely and cozy, like a dream, and before I knew it I fell asleep against my mother's soft shoulder.

Sixteen

I woke up surrounded by a pile of sheets, with Sally's elbow poking me in the neck. I pushed her and the sheets away and rolled off Ma's pullout couch. It was dawn, and the pinky purple sky outside soothed me a little. Every part of my body hurt. It was like I had been swimming through a rough tide the whole day before. I didn't think I had the energy for a day at the beach. I wanted to roll back into bed, but I needed to be alone. One cock crowed, and then another. I knew this was probably the only chance I would get today to be by myself.

I washed up and pulled a pair of shortalls over the T-shirt I had slept in. As I got ready to tiptoe outside, I looked at Sally asleep on the couch and realized that the news about my father couldn't have been easy for her, either. She could have easily ratted me out to Ma or to our parents once she knew what I was really up to, but she never did. Ma said that when she came back to the house the second time I had snuck off to see Brother John, Sally had tried to cover for me and said that Raj and I were out on an errand for his mother. But when we hadn't shown up another hour later, that excuse was worn thin. Then she covered for me again when Dad asked if Mitch was coming to the party. That was a huge risk. I dipped into my bag and pulled out my notepad. I doodled a drawing of her birthmark, the butterfly queen, rising off her arm. I wrote "thanks" at the bottom, and left it folded on the coffee table where she would see it as soon as she woke up. Then I snuck out, being careful of the creaky front door.

There was a surprising chill in the air, and dew glistened on the grass and leaves. All the flowers were just beginning to uncoil their petals and open to the morning sun. I had never known flowers could close up for the night the way they did here. There was so much I hadn't known before coming to Trinidad. I stepped out onto the cold concrete stairs in my bare feet and shivered slightly, as Haysley looked up at me and yawned from his spot on the third step.

"Good morning, Hays."

He licked his choppers in response.

"Wanna go for a walk?"

Hays stood up and stretched his front legs and back flat out, yawning all the while. Then he followed me out the gate. We walked down the hill, toward the smell of freshly baked bread. My stomach began to grumble and I wished I had thought to bring some money. I didn't want to go back now. Ma was probably up already, and I wasn't ready to face my family. As Hays and I rounded the corner, going around some bushes at an empty lot, I spotted Raj coming out of the bakery. He smiled and waved.

"You up real early."

"You too."

"My mother sent me to get *hops* for breakfast." He opened the bag, and the bread, still hot from the oven, released a waft of delicious steam into the air. "You hungry?"

I nodded. We walked back into the bakery, and he bought six more. Hays devoured his bread in one chomp. I was almost as ravenous and finished one roll by the time we were halfway back up the hill. I fed Haysley another and pulled my second helping out as the last cock finished his morning crowing.

"My parents know that I found out."

Raj nodded as he chewed.

"My mom's okay but my dad's furious. I figured they were going to be mad at me for finding out. I thought they might ground me or something, but the look on my dad's face—he's so much more angry than that."

We had come to Ma's gate, but I wasn't ready to go inside. The kitchen window shutters were open, and steam streamed out. "Aunty Jackie's going to be here soon, and it'll be time to leave. I don't think I want to go after all."

We sat in the grass and leaned against Ma's cold concrete fence. Thankfully the sun was beginning to warm everything up. "I thought I was going to be so angry at my mom for not telling me anything, for making me go through all of this to find out about my father, but she was so sorry she hadn't told me before. She looked really sad, Raj. I felt so selfish for ever thinking she was just being mean. And she told me what all the stuff in the box was. You should see my father's drawings.

They're really good! I wish I were that good."

"You draw pretty good too."

"Not like that. But anyway, he seemed really great. My mom said that he was such a nice guy, and he was a terrific soccer player, and that he was going to the university here to become a lawyer. So he was smart, too." I ripped some grass from the ground. "I wish I'd known him. I just found him, and he's not even here. I think I should feel bad, like I should cry because he's dead, but I don't know him at all. How can I cry over someone I don't even know? And then if I do, does that mean my dad will get even more angry? You should have seen how he made my mom look last night." Even though I thought I couldn't, I cried then. Raj leaned over and patted my unruly hair. I realized with a slight pang that I hadn't even tried to comb my hair that morning, and that it must have looked like an enormous autumn bush, but he didn't seem to care, so maybe I shouldn't have either. Besides, my hair was just like my father's.

"Rajindra?" It was Raj's mother. She was standing in the street with both hands on her hips. "We waiting on you for breakfast, you know?"

Raj looked at the bag of bread in his hand and struggled to his feet. "Sorry, Mummy."

"It was my fault, Mrs. Seepersad," I said. "I made him stop."

She shook her head. "That's all right. But we need to get something to eat. You too," she said to me. "Time to go inside."

Raj followed his mother into their yard, and Hays and I went inside Ma's. My dad was leaning over the porch railing with a mug of hot coffee. My stomach knotted with fear. I closed the porch gate, leaving Haysley to chase his tail and then settle into a ball on the top step. I turned to face my dad.

"Hey."

He nodded, still looking over to the other side of the street. "So you just walk out of the house in the morning without telling anybody?"

"Sorry. But I didn't go far."

"That's not the point. Nobody knew where you were."

"Well, I didn't see anybody come looking for me."

Dad turned his head to look at me. I stepped back and leaned against the gate. "You went out in the street like that with nothing on your feet? You trying to catch a cold? Look, just go inside and clean up, please. Your grandmother has your breakfast on the table, and your aunt will be here just now."

I stepped forward, staying close to the wall opposite him, and began to make my way softly inside. As I got to the door, I turned back around.

"Why are you so mad at me?" My voice was high. It didn't sound like my own.

"I asked you to go in and get cleaned up, Grace." He didn't sound angry then, just tired. His head hung low, nearly touching his mug.

"Please. I know you're mad at me. I can tell."

Dad sank down into the nearest chair, and shook his head. "I'm not mad at you, Grace. I love you. I'm just sad."

"Why?"

"You're too young to understand, Grace."

"I'm not too young," I said, stamping my foot on the floor. "You and mom always say that, but I'm not. I can understand if you explain it to me. You're always saying I'm so smart. If I'm so smart, then why don't you think I'd understand?"

"Okay, it's like this. You and I are family. It's because I chose you, not because you were mine to begin with. I always worked hard to make sure you knew how much you were loved because I knew that someday you would realize I was just a stand-in. You would resent me for trying to be someone I wasn't. And now you're growing up so fast, Grace. You won't even be my little girl anymore. You'll go off to college in a few years and then, if you know that I'm not your daddy, well, then I'm not anybody. I didn't want you to know. I was afraid I'd lose you."

"You thought that if I found out about my other father that I would be mad at you? How could I be? You're the dad I grew up with, the one from all my first memories. That's real. I know it."

"Grace, I—"

"Nobody can take your place, Dad. Even if my other father was still alive, you're still my dad."

"Grace," he said, shaking his head. He couldn't continue. I walked over and hugged him. He brushed a tear from his face with the back of his hand. "You're right. I guess I was just—afraid. You never should have found out this way, baby. It wasn't right. I made it hard for your mother. I know that now. I'm sure I made it hard for you, too. Like that night we took Sally to the hospital. You remember that night?"

"I remember."

"I was so mad that you knew anything about him. I thought

it was the beginning of the end for us. I thought I'd never have my little girl ever again."

"That's not how it was, Dad."

"It's just hard when you feel like you don't belong to someone that you love so much."

"I know exactly what you mean, Dad. Sometimes I feel like that too."

"But why, Gracie?"

I hesitated and tried to step back, but he held on to my hands. "You and Sally really belong to each other. I don't. I'm always on the outside."

"That isn't how I feel, Gracie. You and Sally are both my girls. I love you both the same."

"But we never do stuff together like you and Sally do."

"You quit the soccer team just after I started to coach. And you like to write and draw. Those don't really require team participation. But I tell you what, we'll try to spend some Daddy and Gracie time. How about it? We can go to the MoMA. I know it's your favorite museum."

"Yeah, okay. Thanks, Dad."

He stood up and ruffled my already messy hair. "Go get some breakfast. We have a long day ahead."

As I stepped inside Sally was patting the couch pillows back into place. Our blankets were neatly folded on the coffee table. "You didn't have to do that by yourself, Sal. I would have helped you."

She pulled my note out of her pocket. "I think we're even," she said.

* * *

I slept the entire ride to Maracas Beach. When we got there, Mom shook me awake. I plopped down on a beach towel and propped myself up against the trunk of a coconut tree. I bit happily into the salty-sweet skin of a preserved prune and looked around me. Curved behind me were hills that rose straight up to the sky, covered with tropical plants that had leaves so big Sally and I could use them as blankets. Brightly plumed birds soared above me and swerved between branches and hanging vines. In front of me the beige sand and the blue sea gleamed like jewel-encrusted satin. And the sky above it all was bright and clear.

Everyone was there, playing on the sand, eating, splashing, laughing, but I just wanted to sit in the shade. I laughed out loud as Raj and Shankar dunked Sally under a wave. Suddenly I realized someone was watching me. I looked up to find Brother John with a familiar-looking red-haired young woman.

"Hi," I said as I got up to shake his hand. "I didn't think you were coming after all," I said nervously. I looked around for my dad.

"We had to meet at least one more time, Grace." He gestured to the woman next to him. "And besides, I brought a friend."

"I remember you," I said. "I ran into you on the street."

She laughed. "Yes, you did. Hello."

"You're a friend of Brother John's?"

She glanced sideways at Brother John and smiled nervously. "Actually, I'm Angél's sister. I'm your aunt. I came to meet you at the mall, but you left before I got the chance."

"Why didn't you tell me?" I asked Brother John.

"Some things are better when they unfold on their own. Now you've spoken to your parents about everything, and you probably feel a lot better than you did back then, so it's the perfect time for you two to meet, not so?"

I wondered how he knew that I'd talked to my parents, and then I saw them looking at us from a few coconut trees down. Dad didn't look upset that Brother John was there, and Mom smiled and waved. I waved back. "I guess it is."

"So, Grace, meet your aunt Ava. Ava, this is Grace."

She pounced on me immediately, like she had only been waiting for permission to squeeze the living daylights out of me. "I didn't know. I never knew about you. You're so beautiful. She looks so much like Angél, no?" she said to Brother John.

He nodded quietly. "I'll give you two a moment," he said, and strolled off across the sand, with his dreadlocked hair and long clothes blowing behind him in the breeze.

"I brought you something," Aunt Ava said. She pulled a large brown envelope out of her beach bag and settled down on the towel next to me. "I keep these with me wherever I am. They help keep Angél close to my heart." She opened the envelope and pulled out letters, all written by my father, and a few family photos. "I was very young when Angél came here to go to the university, but he always wrote to me to let me know that even though he was far away, he was still looking out for me. The letters had little drawings all over them that illustrated what he was writing about—his classes, playing soccer, even going out with my mom.

"I do that," I told her. "I doodle all over everything too."

"You do? You probably have so many things in common."

"Like what?"

"Well, I don't know." She looked up at a nearby vendor. "You want an ice cream? It's so hot."

I followed her to the stand, and we got two cones. "I'll have soursop," I said when the vendor asked for my flavor.

"That was Angél's favorite too."

"Really?"

She raised her eyebrows and nodded. "Our mother used to make it from scratch. Angél would get soursop off the tree in our yard and beg our mother to make it for him. He could eat a whole batch by himself. When they were in season, she would be making batches of soursop ice cream almost every day!"

"Really? What else?"

Aunt Ava and I stood in the shade of a small grove of coconut trees, and I listened as she told story after story about my father as a boy growing up in Venezuela. So much of what she described sounded just like me.

"But you know, if you want to know more, you will have to ask your grandmother."

"You mean Ma?"

"No, I mean my mother, your grandmother in Venezuela. She has a lot more stories than I do."

"I never even thought about having a whole other family."

"You do, and they would love to meet you."

"How many of them are there?"

"We have a big family, Grace. You're just going to have to come to Venezuela to meet them all yourself. We'll talk to your parents about that, okay?"

I nodded.

"Oh, my goodness," Aunt Ava exclaimed. "Look!" She held her hand out and pulled a ring off her finger. She put it on my hand and it clicked into the ring from my mother's box. Now the flower was complete, and a little hummingbird hovered over it, sipping nectar. "When Mitch sent my brother's things back to Venezuela, this was with them. I didn't realize until just now what it belonged to. I think it was meant to stay together, no?"

"No, Aunty," I said. "You and I are family. We'll both wear a piece." I handed back her part of the ring, and she slipped it on her finger. "I think that's how it's meant to be."

Mom came over then to say hello, and Dad, who had been taking pictures of everyone at the party, ran over to snap a shot of the three of us, me standing in the middle, with my arms around my mother and my aunt. The three of us fit together like puzzle pieces. I felt very, very good.

Seventeen

A week later I sat looking out the airplane window as the whole of Trinidad shrunk beneath me. The airport grew small, then nearby fields with cows grazing on beautiful green grass appeared and shrunk. Colorful houses, low buildings, streets with cars driving on the wrong side of the road appeared in the window and got farther and farther away. Soon all I could make out were colors— brown and red, and shades of rich deep greens, then sparkling blue. In the distance a brown landmass appeared on the horizon. Venezuela. We flew into a thick white cloud, and suddenly both Trinidad and Venezuela were gone. And just like that, I wished I were back in Ma's yard with the *zaboca* tree and the hibiscus bushes. I could smell Haysley's damp fur and feel the warmth of the ground rising up beneath my feet. My mind drifted to the warm sand on Maracas Beach, my aunt Ava, and going to meet Grandma Maria next summer. I wondered what her house looked like. I wondered if she had a *zaboca* tree. I reached into my bag and pulled out the pocket English/Spanish dictionary that Raj bought me as a good-bye gift. I looked up the translation for "dog." *"Perro,"* I said aloud. Maybe she had an old dog like Hays too.

Sally giggled next to me. *"Perro,"* she repeated, rolling her *r*s perfectly. "You think that dogs in Venezuela say 'rrruf, rrruf,' instead of 'ruff, ruff'?" she asked with an extra giggle.

"Rrruf," I said, giggling too.

I wished Raj could hear me. Just a few hours before, we were sitting in front of Ma's house, looking up words in Spanish and practicing saying them out loud.

"I can e-mail you from the computer at the *biblioteca,*" he said. He pointed out where he had written his e-mail address in the front pages of the dictionary as he flicked that lock of hair out of his eyes for probably the last time. His mother had promised that she would take him for a haircut as soon as we drove away. We sat on Ma's front steps while everyone else piled bags into Aunty Jackie's trunk and did a last check of the house, not willing to say good-bye to each other yet. But when the time came to leave, Raj leaned over and quickly kissed me on the lips. I sat shocked as he smiled his good-bye and went back to his own yard. Just when I thought I had all the surprises I could have handled that summer, there was another. Aunty Jackie came just then, as I was trying to catch my breath, and she ushered me to the car, where I piled into the backseat with Sally and Mom and our carry-on bags. I waved to Ma and Raj and the yellow house, until all three disappeared behind a growth of thick wild bush as we turned the corner by the bakery.

I had missed my friends in Brooklyn so much over the

summer. I wondered how hard it was going to be not seeing my new friend over the whole school year before I came back to Trinidad next summer. And even then, I would be splitting my time between Trinidad and Venezuela, so we probably would only see each other for about a month. I looked at Raj's e-mail address again. I would e-mail him at least once a week.

As I put the dictionary away, a couple of pictures fell out of my bag. I picked them up and dealt them out on my tray table. They were the beach photos from Aunty Jackie's album, some from my mother's memory box, and a couple of the ones that my dad had taken on the beach. I overlapped them so that I had one long picture of all my family and friends together. In the middle of them all was the blurred picture that had started my whole adventure, and next to it was the picture Dad had taken of Mom, Aunt Ava, and me. They were very similar. There was Mom, smiling the same smile from the right side of both photos, my aunt Jackie on the left in the old photo, and my aunt Ava taking that spot in the new one. And in the center of both photos was a redhead with a birthmark. I put my hand on my birthmark and imagined that I was having a moment with my father.

I played around with all the pictures until I formed an image of my mom, my dad, my birth father, Sally, and me. We all seemed to be standing on the same stretch of beach. I put the rest of the pictures away and stared at the picture I had created of my real family. In it, my father had one eye clicked down into a wink. I winked back. Of all the secrets that had been formed and revealed this summer, I was happy to get to the bottom of each of them—my birth father, my dad's fear, my first kiss. I realized that not all secrets are the kind that turns your whole world upside down. Some of them are sweet little things that are simply too delicious to let slip.

About the Author

Tracey Baptiste was born in Trinidad. She has been making up stories for as long as anyone in her family can remember. When she was twelve, she wrote a short novel about two friends who moved to New York. Three years later she moved with her family to Brooklyn, New York. But she goes back to Trinidad often so she can lie in the sand at Maracas Beach.

A former elementary school teacher, she now lives with her husband and daughter in Englewood, New Jersey. You can visit her Web site at www.traceybaptiste.com.

Of *Angel's Grace*, Han Nolan said, "[It] kept me turning the pages until the very end." Jerdine Nolen called it a work "full of grace and forgiveness."

Ms. Baptiste is at work on a new novel.